The Poet and the Donkey

Books by May Sarton

The Poet and
the Donkey

by MAY SARTON

Illustrations by Stefan Martin

W · W · NORTON & COMPANY · *New York · London*

First published as a Norton paperback 1984

Copyright © 1969 by May Sarton

Library of Congress Catalog Card No. 72-80024

ISBN 393-30159-1

All Rights Reserved

Published simultaneously in Canada by
George J. McLeod Limited, Toronto

Printed in the United States of America

3 4 5 6 7 8 9 0

For Eleanor Blair

CONTENTS

Chaque journée est plus émouvante et nouvelle . . .
Mais pourquoi ceuillez-vous ces roses, ces mortelles?
Qu'espérez-vous de laisser ici de plus vivant?
—Gardons-nous d'abîmer la divine Figure!
Qu'en notre absence soit toute chose aussi pure,
Toute chose aussi belle et triste qu'a présent;

Que je puisse remettre entre tes mains très sages
Une existence unie, intacte, à ton image;
Que ta création, mon Dieu, ne porte pas
La trace de ce corps ardent et délectable,
De ces pas, au hasard, égarés sur le sable,
Ces pas désespérés, cette chute,—et ces pas . . .

—Odilon-Jean Périer
from "La Route"

The Poet and the Donkey

Andy Lightfoot and the Muse

CHAPTER 1

It had been a hard spring for Andy Lightfoot. For one thing it had rained all through June; for another he had lost his Muse, and this is a serious blow to a poet who is not so young as he once was. Chewing a piece of grass and noting that the Oriental poppies were rotting in their buds, Andy reckoned that a poet without a Muse is like a man who has hurt his thumb—everything becomes a little harder to manage. That's what I mean, Andy said to himself, as he nearly slipped on the steep stone steps down into the garden. It was unfair that this particular thing should have happened to him this rainy summer.

However preposterous she had been, the Muse had stayed by him through three long years. For three years poems had accompanied him, lines had run through his head all unasked while he puttered about, chopping wood, shoveling snow, gardening, and Musing. It was all he could do to keep up with the poems. If he decided to go for a short drive and really wanted to be alone, they pursued him down the road, and sometimes he had to stop the car to jot down a line. His head was full of a musical buzz, and although his Muse had chosen to inhabit an odd and inappropriate person, Andy Lightfoot was happy because he was writing poems and that is what he was meant to do.

He was a small man, but lately he had begun to put on weight—a sure sign of grief—so he looked stout, a stout little man with a shock of white hair, bright blue eyes, and a crooked mouth that sometimes opened into a wide beaming smile. In his plaid shirts, dungarees, and moccasins, he looked like anybody else around the village, at least at a first glance. At a second glance a person might wonder, might think he looked more like a hunter than a farmer, very quiet and alert, more wide awake than most. There was a keen edge in him somewhere. If he looked at a person, that person might feel forced to look away, as if he were being discovered. But by now the people in the village took him for granted, even to his silences and his unwillingness to be dragged into whatever social life there was. He had become part of the natural landscape, like his house and its weathered clapboards, bright red door, and big chimney. His neighbors were not readers of poetry and had no inkling that, as far as the world outside went, they had rather a rare bird in their midst and some people would give a good deal to meet this shy, stout, bright-eyed woodcock of a man. For outside the village, in public libraries strewn over the country, Andy Lightfoot had many friends. Young boys and old ladies carried poems of his in their pockets, and even the critics gave an occasional two cheers (although never three) when his books appeared at long intervals.

But very few people indeed had any idea what his life was really all about, nor what he meant exactly when he mentioned the Muse, nor could he have explained. A Muse is a hard companion to handle at best. She is never quite human, as Andy had learned over the years, but she inhabits a human being, and as long as she does, that human being dazzles the eyes. That person haunts, troubles, delights and appalls without even trying. And all around her there is a strong magnetic field.

So, Andy sometimes thought, it is rather like having a living ghost at your side all the time. Three years ago when the Muse became so obsessive that he was unable to go out for a quiet drive without her badgering him, he had chuckled as he remembered a tale an old lady had told him about a little girl who was heard saying to her dog, "Go home, Lolly! It's bad enough having God around all the time, without your following me, too, wherever I go!"

But if Andy had chuckled then, when poems flowed through him and he hardly had time or energy to get them fashioned, he tore out a handful of weeds now with something like rage, and when he looked up at the rich June greens all around him, he felt stifled.

It is all very well, he thought, for a young man to lose a Muse. When Andy was twenty, they came a dime a dozen, and almost any pretty girl dazzled for a brief moment. When he was young, the Muse might even inhabit a tree or a wave just breaking. He was always, then, glimpsing the hem of her garment, evanescent in the foam. He could pick up a worn stone on the beach, or a sand dollar, and fall into a fit of concentration. But when one is close to sixty, the Muse is not so easy to catch. Her appearances are rare, and a really long Musing, such as he had just experienced, is a great and splendid gift from life.

He could see now how wrong he had been to complain when she did not answer the poems he sent her, or the books, when they came out dedicated to her—in her human guise, of course—or the flowers, such as red roses at Christmas. For he saw now that the Muse had, on the whole, been kind. Silence has its point. Silence, like a sky of stars on a winter night, is full of mystery and elevation. Words, on the other hand, can kill. It is very bad when the Muse misspells a poet's name, for instance. And that she had done. In a rare written word she had called him "Sandy," and for some days after that Andy felt strangely shaken, as if his very existence were being subtly undermined.

Nervous and on edge, he had then made a fatal mistake. He had tried to pin the Muse down. This is one thing a poet must not do, because he should know that magic cannot be pinned down and that is why it is magic. Worse, in order to pin her down, Andy had turned to an infernal machine, the telephone. A disembodied voice, called out of the air, may sound like an oracle even when all it says is the state of the weather, but intoxicating as this form of communication was at first, it could only end badly. When the power of the Muse began to disappear like the Cheshire Cat, leaving only an ironic smile floating in the air between them, and when the tide of poems began to ebb, Andy made a wild gamble, and tried to speak to her again. This time it was not to make a little magic weather happen, but to force the issue, and to ask for a half-hour interview. A half hour with the Muse, he imagined, might have turned the tide and given him three more years on a rising flood of poems. It was a desperate gamble.

When gamblers lose they are supposed to take it well if they are gentlemen, but no good poet is a gentleman, and Andy took his loss badly. He entirely forgot all the good advice he gave to others when they came to him with their problems, the gist being that if you wait a while and are patient, things generally get better rather than worse. No, he did none of these things he should have done. He brooded. He developed symptoms. They were comparable to the symptoms a garden suffers when there is a drought. First, the flowers become pindling and even dry in their buds, then the leaves begin to wilt, and finally, if the drought is prolonged, their roots, finding no nourishment, die.

Andy woke up in the morning, that spring, and did not greet the new day with a happy think about all the things he planned to do. He wanted to turn his face to the wall, but was unable to because one of the cats would be sure to come and scratch his nose with a starfish paw, and that meant, "Where is my breakfast, you lazy sailor?" Andy was not so far gone that such a plea could go unanswered, especially when it was brown-and-gold and soft-as-plush Pussel who made it. But after the cats' breakfast, he had to face his own. And his own breakfast, even when it was kippered herring and a corn muffin, made him feel rather sick. He had not slept well. Poets without a Muse sleep fitful sleeps and have nightmares. Twice Andy dreamt that a horse was eating his hand, and once that he himself was drowning in a well.

He began to have a peculiar stifled feeling in his chest. More than once, confronted with an imitation poem he was concocting out of bits and pieces, without the fertilizing influence, he had a dizzy spell at his desk. And by the end of June it was clear that he was in a bad way. But, however crazy he had become since the Muse took off, he was not so crazy that he thought any of these symptoms had a physical cause that a medical man might be able to cure. Muses do not come in bottles marked "Take morning and evening. This prescription cannot be renewed."

No, what he needed was something, someone, who would again capture his whole attention, if not a new Muse (heaven forbid, he thought, for he was loyal) then something that could change the inner atmosphere, bring in some fresh air. But what? Or how? He had lived in this village now for fifteen years and knew it by heart. True, he had friends—there was Trumbull Hare, who lived in a henhouse down the road opposite the formidable Miss Pickthorn, and Trumbull Hare's dog, Crackerjack, was a frequent visitor, as regular as the mailman on his morning and evening rounds. Andy gave him three dog biscuits whenever he chose to call, and in return Trumbull Hare sometimes left Andy a rainbow trout wrapped in a young bracken leaf. There was Mrs. Dear across the green a piece, and the Crocker clan waved as they went past. But he did not see any potential muses among these neighbors. Perhaps the Muse must be more than, as well as in some ways less than, human, and his friends around here were just plain human.

What was he going to do with himself?

He Remembers Miss Hornbeam

CHAPTER 2

It still rained nearly every day, and Andy, gloomy and self-devouring, sat at his desk and chewed the cud of memory. Since there was no Muse, he rehearsed what she had been, wondered why she was as she was, and considered how it had all happened. He did this to ward off panic, for it was a strange and frightening state to be in when words did not come to his mind, when there was no echo, when he thought and thought and nothing whatever happened, except a few squiggles he made into elephants or daisies with his new pen.

The two cats, speckled brown and gold, padded about like children who don't know what to do with themselves, subdued by the rain. Sneakers, who managed to look like a kitten although she was nearly ten years old, took to sleeping on his desk. At least, then, there was someone to talk to, for when she heard Andy's voice, she purred even though fast asleep.

"I'm getting awfully old, Sneakers," he explained, "and I feel baffled."

Gentle purr.

"I do wish this pain in my chest would go away."

Loud purr. One golden eye opened for a moment, and one paw stretched out, then she curled the paw round her nose and slept.

Andy sat and remembered. He held the faint memory of oceans in his heart as in an empty shell, and he listened, listened, as if he might catch once more the haunting roar of the receding wave.

Like all poets, Andy earned a precarious living. "Poems don't sell," Gary Snyder had snarled when Andy took back the few remaining volumes of his *Selected Poems* from the counter of the General Store. They were replaced by balloons, chewing gum, and cigars, and "good riddance" was in Snyder's cold eye as he handed the books over.

There was no possible answer, of course. Poems did not sell. But, fortunately poets can make a partial living these days by reading at colleges and universities, and in this Andy was no exception. He was apt to "go out," as he put it, for a few weeks in the spring, and again in the fall. It was on one of these journeys, three years before, that the Muse swam into his ken—a journey, in this instance, to a college only two hundred miles away, where he was to read and also address two classes. It was in December, but there had been an April sky that day, bursts of light, dark clouds, and unseasonal warmth in the air. Andy, childishly susceptible to atmosphere, felt happy and elated, and decided on an impulse to attend chapel at eleven, before the luncheon in his honor at the President's house. He had not gone to college—he had spent what would have been his college years flat on his back, in and out of hospitals, with tuberculosis of the spine. So he observed college life with a peculiar nostalgia, mixed with amusement. Professors, especially professors in a girls' school such as this, seemed to him rare creatures, rare and delightful, like some strange species found only in a zoo. He observed them and had a longing to tease, a longing which he quelled because he was a shy creature himself. And also because he felt humble before all he imagined they had in their distinguished, but so rarely beautiful, heads. With the students, on the other hand, he was perfectly at home. They were as naked and vulnerable as he. They were full of merriment, and laughed reassuringly at his jokes. Also they listened. They listened with their whole hearts, and so—they heard.

Andy loved ceremony. He loved the ceremony of tennis or baseball. He loved formal places where people look suddenly beautiful because they are coming down a stone stairway to a fountain, and he loved the ceremony of chapel in a small college. That day he took his place at the back of the severe white hall where the long rectangular windows let in a lot of sky and framed the naked branches of the maples. He watched the choir file in, and listened to the hymns and the invocation in a state of transparent passivity. He felt he was floating on the music, empty for once of sensation, tremor, apprehension, or guilt.

And then it happened. Miss Hornbeam, the President, stood up in her black gown and quaint mortarboard, and talked to the students. What did she talk about? Andy could not remember. He had not, in any case, heard what she *said*. He had heard the extraordinary rumor inside his head, and what he had seen was not Miss Hornbeam but the Muse. Whatever is this about? he had asked himself. What is happening to me now?

Of course he had no recollection that this was exactly how he had felt when he met Charity, twenty years before, picking up shells on a beach and she lifted her small golden head and smiled. He did not remember that this was exactly how he had felt when he caught Olivia's eye at a café table in Paris, long after Charity had married someone else. Olivia was ten years older than he and very much married but, willy-nilly, she became the Muse, for the Muse tends to inhabit inappropriate people more often than not. She comes without warning, as an entirely fresh and overwhelming sensation, so Andy, sitting in the hard pew, did not relate what was happening to him to anything that had ever happened before.

In between these mysterious apparitions, there had been other girls with whom he fell in love. For Andy had a tender heart and a loving nature. He had always felt it was mere chance that he had not married, but perhaps this too was part of the plan to keep him writing poems, for that was what he was meant to do. Whatever Andy knew or did not know, he did know that he was destined to be a servant and not a master. And those soft white girls on whose breasts he had lain his head for a month or a year were not to be his forever, nor to appease the hunger in his heart.

He walked over to the President's house smiling with pleasure at crossing the still-green campus among so many ravishing girls, and he went garlanded in their answering smiles up to the forbidding front door, and he rang the bell as innocent as the day.

He was placed, as guest of honor, on Miss Hornbeam's right hand. On his right was a brilliant creature with flashing blue eyes and such aggressive self-assurance as made Andy fold in his horns and vanish into his shell. From there he heard her bombard him with questions that he could sense were barbed, such as why he chose to write in form, but since she was not very much interested in his answers, he murmured a little nonsense and left it at that. His mind was elsewhere—on Miss Hornbeam's face when he dared to look at it. For, in his inner person, he was already unfolding this face like a map which must quickly be learned by heart, so that he could decipher it later.

Miss Hornbeam was still rather young to be a President, and although she controlled everything within her orbit with a determined and masterful hand, she could not control her charm. So when she turned on him her usual polite smile, the effect was as if the glasses around the table had suddenly become musical glasses, and Andy listened to her perfunctory queries with a third ear that translated them into mysterious words, the words of an oracle.

"What do I do?" He turned the question over in his mind. "You mean, all day?"

What did he do? In the light of Miss Hornbeam's dark eye, he was aware that he did absolutely nothing, nothing whatever. He did not attend committee meetings; he did not gather trustees together and lay great plans before them; he did not cope with recalcitrant students; he did not decide to open one road and close another at a cost of half a million dollars, or to plant trees where there were none; he did not dictate vast quantities of letters to a secretary.

Unfortunately, there was a silence round the table as she asked her question, so the question took on a little more than its light weight was meant to carry.

"Well . . ." Andy twisted round the glass in front of him. "I lie in wait for poems, I guess. At my age they are rare, as rare as migrating Canada geese."

"They are seasonal?" Miss Hornbeam asked, with evident amusement. "Spring and fall?"

"Then what happens in winter and summer?" Miss Self-assurance chimed in.

"I putter around," Andy answered, as if the question had been meant seriously. "I have a garden. It's hard work keeping it going. And in winter, I read, shovel snow, put out seed for the birds, keep the woodpile going." His eyes rested for a fleeting moment on Miss Hornbeam's hand, crumbling a cracker. "Mostly I'm considering things— things that might be poems and often, these days, turn out to be elusive."

"It sounds like heaven," Miss Hornbeam murmured.

What a kind person she must be, he thought gratefully, for he had never felt more foolish in his life.

"Once in a while a poem really comes out, but that's rare these days. You, I presume, can hope to finish what you begin?"

"Not always," and Miss Hornbeam took in the table's attention with a charming light laugh. "We are in a hassle right now about the new curriculum. Some of us don't believe it will ever get cleared away. But I am an optimist, unlike most of my faculty."

"You exert a strong spell to make things happen."

"Spell?" She looked quite startled for a second, then turned toward Andy with an air of closing the door firmly on personal remarks. "I try to keep cool and keep at it."

But Andy was now too absorbed in trying to encompass Miss Hornbeam's world to notice. "Yes, I can see how it might be rather like a beaver making a dam."

The remark caused general amusement, and Andy felt he was outside a secret society where he would always just miss the point, even to the lightness of Miss Hornbeam's tone that managed to conceal the truth Andy was after, the truth of the person inside the administrator.

"I feel more often like an inept juggler," she answered, "trying to keep a dozen plates in the air. . . . One is always slipping out of my hands."

"Such as a million dollars for a faculty club?" Miss Self-assurance asked.

"Oh, that plate is still in the air!"

Andy had to concentrate hard, like a person swimming under water, simply to appear to be normal and not utter some violent cry of joy and relief as the Muse's strong magic began to work.

Food was placed before him and he ate of it as if it were celestial bread. Around him the talk buzzed on. He was grateful to be left alone and to listen to it from a very great distance, the murmur of human voices in which his own joined now and then, equally irrelevant.

Only at the end Miss Hornbeam's voice reached him with devastating effect and pierced him awake as she expressed regret that she would be unable to hear his reading. "I have a meeting of the Board of Trustees," she explained, perhaps felt compelled to explain, before the naked desolation in his glance.

"It has been a momentous occasion," he said as she shook hands at the door, but already her mind was elsewhere, and perhaps she did not hear, or had been irritated by the use of such a strong word for a rather dull luncheon party.

The great heavy door swung to behind him, and he stood on the steps a moment, in dismay. How could he ever manage to see her again? Andy was innocent, but he had lived a good many years and, as a visiting bard, had observed a good many college presidents, and he was not so innocent as to imagine that this sort of person was easy to communicate with on a purely human level. If, for instance, he could have given the college a million dollars, or even half a million, he might dare ask her out to dinner and she might accept, but he suspected that this would be the only possible ploy. His bank balance was about a thousand at the moment, and that was more than he usually had. It would clearly not be enough, even if he lived on bread and water for a year.

He must have walked away in his distress and excitement, for after a time he found himself standing by a small lily pond in front of a modern building, and looking down at his own face reflected in its dark surface. What he saw dismayed him. It was a ludicrously different image from that which he carried inside him, this image of an elderly professor on his way to a class.

We have to break the mirrors to be ourselves, he thought, throwing a pebble in and watching the image blur and vanish—especially when we are over forty. "We have to break the mirrors to be ourselves," he murmured, aware that it was a line in iambic pentameter. He tasted it. He examined it. He wondered whether it would be more accurate to write it "to become ourselves," but that did not scan. "We have to break the mirrors to become . . ." —maybe. Already the Muse was at work. The true sign of her spell would always be the arrival out of the blue of complete lines of poems, and the horror of her absence was that, without her, he was forced to write entirely in free verse.

How to explain it? —An electric current turned on. By the time he stood up to read before a gathering of English majors, he had roughed out the first stanza of the first true poem he had been given in years. So, it was beginning again, the tremendous elation, the sense of being commanded by forces over which he had no control, the furious hopes, the denials and self-denials, the concentrated hours when he sometimes threw away a hundred versions in the hammering-out of a short lyric, the sense of everything he knew and felt and had become up to that moment fusing at last into a piece of created magic.

He could hardly wait to get home, and there in his silence, so alive again, feel his way into the new poems. By the time he left the college his pockets were full of envelopes and the backs of matchbooks with ideas and lines jotted down on them, light-hearted attacks on the great closed door of the Muse. For everything, of course, was pivoted around her, and was written for her, whether she ever read it or not. See it as a tightrope, Andy thought, a tension that could bear his full weight at last. He was on his feet and dancing again, instead of sitting with a piece of slack rope in his hands wondering where on earth or heaven to attach it.

The excitement came partly from a ruthless self-examination in the light of Miss Hornbeam's eyes, a renewal from being stretched into such a foreign country as hers must be to him. And it came partly from the leap of imagination to join her there, to take in, absorb, probe, come to understand, just what her life must be like. Lonely, he murmured, it was bound to be, but not so much lonely for someone else (he had no illusions) as for the human self she must bury so much of the time. And that was where he might—oh, he surely could—be of use.

Within weeks he had sent ten poems off to the office of the President, and the long, the interminable, wait began. If he had suspected from the first that from this Muse there could be no quick answer, this is what reason told him, but reason had very little to do with the experience of Musing. Must not a poet hunt the unicorn through bush and bramble, through snow and fire, over desert and mountain, through thickets and over long barren roads, even though he suspects sometimes that the unicorn does not exist—or exists only in his imagination?

One night in January when there was a full moon, so bright that Andy amused himself by writing on a moonlit page, he suddenly decided to use the telephone to get through that closed door. If the telephone is an infernal machine, rousing the unwilling listener out of sleep or work, relentless interrupter, imposing a human voice on a silence, yet it is also sometimes a magic machine that brings a dear unexpected voice into the room from a great distance away, as if a living bird had lighted on a head or hand.

It was rather a shock to discover that he had to reach Miss Hornbeam through the barrage of a college operator, who forwarded his name to the invisible and inaudible Muse to await her Yes or No. This time she answered.

"Yes, Mr. Lightfoot?"

Crisp, impatient Miss Hornbeam had the grace to answer.

"There is a full moon. I just hoped you had time to take a look."

"Thank you"—she was surprised into a gentle laugh. "I was working. I am making a hard decision. I'll look at the moon, Mr. Lightfoot. Perhaps it will help."

"I am writing a hard poem," he said.

"Good to know that someone else is struggling away so late tonight."

"Good hunting, Miss Hornbeam!"

As he put the receiver down, such happiness flooded him that he put on snowshoes and went for a short walk in the woods, where the crisscross of small tree shadows made it all look like a scrambled sheet of music. So she is there and I am here, he thought, and it is enough. But that was because he had found a way to open the door at last. What purer form could the Muse take, actually, than a disembodied voice across the night? Oracular, haunting . . .

Far far better than the chatter and worldliness of a table in a restaurant and two embodied beings eating and drinking. A voice, a voice in the night! Andy Lightfoot could hardly believe his luck. And for several months, at rare intervals, he opened that door, and heard the magic voice. What she said had very little importance, and perhaps she divined this, for they talked chiefly about the weather, and never once did Andy ask whether she had read the poems.

But of course he thought a great deal about her when he was not writing poems, and about just what made her tick, ring, buzz, or whatever it was she did, almost human, but never quite. He suspected that administrators could not be entirely human in the way a poet must be. They had chosen to cloister the human element in themselves in order to be judicial and impersonal; they could not afford the degree of vulnerability, even childlikeness, that a poet must maintain. It was, then, the tension of opposites that lit up his mind. And where these opposites met was simply in the fact that they were servants of great powers—this was the point of communion between himself and Miss Hornbeam's merry but detached eye— each had set himself apart for a purpose.

Still, Andy had to be very careful to keep any tension out

of these strange conversations by telephone. His value must remain that he, of all people, needed nothing, asked nothing but an abstract moment, a gentle caper through the air, as he trod his tightrope lightly.

But one cold February night when he heard the foxes barking, he lost his balance. He could not remember how he did, nor what he asked, but the answer chilled him to the bone. It was, "As far as I can see I have to be a machine in this job."

A machine . . . a machine . . . He lay awake all night pondering the phrase. For her sake, he felt the bitter cold. He suffered for her, so merry and so wise, and—if this were the truth—so dreadfully imprisoned as a human being. His imagination was wholly engaged in examining what this told him about her, and he launched in the next days on a series of poems addressed to an administrator. It did not occur to him that Miss Hornbeam had meant to warn rather than to reveal. But now when Andy screwed up his courage and asked the college operator for the President's house, he was told on several occasions that she was out, or could not be found, and the operator finally suggested rather sharply that he reach Miss Hornbeam through her secretary in the daytime.

"Whew!" Andy wiped the sweat off his upper lip and swallowed hard. "So that is that."

But what in hell was he to do now? It was not a matter of will after all. He held an absolute trust in his hands not to deny the Muse as long as she chose to communicate with him, via Miss Hornbeam, however recalcitrant Miss Hornbeam proved to be.

Occasionally Pussel made a fat tail and hissed at some

entirely invisible presence, invisible to Andy anyway. More than once, so convincing was her fear, he searched the cupboards and drawers and looked behind doors to find out whether some strange animal might not have got into the house, but he could find nothing. Whatever Pussel saw was not visible to the human eye. So it was with him. The Muse had been visible for an hour in December at a lunch table, then she had been audible for a month or two, and now she had simply vanished. But he was strongly aware of her presence just the same. And she still inhabited his house. As pervasive, as always at his side as the God of the little girl who begged her dog at least to leave her alone, Miss Hornbeam haunted Andy. The tension throughout the long silence became greater rather than less for a whole year, as Andy cast aside all poems dealing directly with the Muse as person and felt himself drawn down to quite another level of discourse, to some inner current or buried river below consciousness where he felt the Muse still spoke to him in a mysterious language that he must answer. This was a new experience, and rather frightening.

For silence was the language, a silence teeming with signs and symbols. And Andy himself was tuned very high, listening for the inaudible and trying to see the invisible reality behind every bush and stone and tree, and in every creak of the house or band of sunlight across the floor.

Early one morning he found a dead owl in the road, still warm. There was no mark of any kind on it. He could lift the huge brown-and-white wing and see the feathers and their exquisite design. He could run a finger over the soft inner lining. And he looked long at the great square head, at the closed eyes. It was piteously soft and disarmed, this bird of prey, even to the strong, pale-yellow legs and ferocious claws hanging limp as he lifted it up and laid it in a bower of soft grasses under a birch tree. When Andy could still talk to the Muse it had been February and the owls were hooting as they called to a mate. Now, in May, this dead one held a message of desolation, of some ardor spent. It made him heartsick. Even a strong drink of Scotch when he got home failed to change the mood. And he did no work that day.

Yet he did not yet despair. As long as he had no sign he still must believe that a message now and then got through. He was sure that it did because he was forced now into a new phase of poems, which he called "Soundings." They were painfully hard to write. It was like trying to break through some inner membrane deep in himself. He often felt as though he were drowning, as in those dreams where one holds one's breath and goes deeper and deeper down into the waters of dream, knowing that to land would be to die, yet that one must land somehow. These dreams end in a gasp that wakes the sleeper. But Andy's waking dream had no such end. It must end in reaching a vision, a reality beyond the reality he knew, and the deeper he went, the more frightening it all became. He was leading a dangerously solitary life, with madness, he sometimes feared, just around the corner. But still he hoped, and still poetry never left his side.

A Person from Porlock

CHAPTER 3

Two years had passed since that fatal telephone call, and several abortive times of hope when Andy imagined that Miss Hornbeam might relent. But by this rainy June, the silence, which had remained alive so long, suddenly went dead. In a way it was interesting, Andy considered, because it proved, so startling and immense was the difference to his whole existence, that it had indeed been alive.

Solitude, rich and magnetic, gave way to loneliness, barren and chilling. And Andy cursed Miss Hornbeam and the Muse for abandoning an old poet to such a plight. Part of the plight was that, because of what he had suffered from that relentless silence, he had sworn that he would never leave a letter unanswered or a person unwelcomed as long as he lived. That was all very well, but, as if to plague him, just that year more people than ever before had felt impelled to write him, to pour out their lives and their problems. When he had been a young man, like all young men Andy had enjoyed setting down all he was doing and thinking in long intimate outpourings to almost anyone—it is one of the ways by which a young man finds out who he is and what he really means. But now that he was nearly sixty and chugged along at a much slower pace at best, letters had become an act of charity by which he responded as best he could to the demands and queries of the young, and also of the old, for, standing in the middle, he was leaned on from both directions, and was now attended by a group of elderly angels who needed him, cherished him, and had grown used to getting a letter from him once a week. As long as he was in touch with the Muse he had carried his correspondence with ease, but now that he was alone and feeling so depressed and seedy, he began to notice that he too was in danger of becoming a machine—a machine for "responding." His desk loomed before him every morning like a prisoner's bench, and it was only out in the garden, in the few bright intervals between rains, that he could forget how frustrated and angry a being he had become.

Weeding was a help. He could curse the weeds without feeling like a criminal character. But he longed sometimes for a feminine presence, for someone to say, "Let's go for a walk, old thing," for someone to make him a baked apple as a surprise, for someone to sew on a button by the fire. He even wondered whether he had made a fatal mistake not to marry years before. There had been Nancy, so cosy and warm, but she had a dreadful way of repeating every-thing he said as if she had to hear it in her own voice to believe it, and he could not have lived with an echo. There had been Susie, black-eyed Susie, so wild and wayward, but she would have let the dishes pile up for a week, and Andy, like all people who live alone, had become per-nickety about things being just so around him. Even a stray spoon could make him feel irritable. No, he decided, I am not the marrying kind because I am the Musing kind and wives are jealous of Muses.

"Besides," he said to Sneakers, who was hoping for a piece of bacon as he stood at the sink washing up after breakfast, "what woman could stand my sudden rages?"

For, exactly like a weather breeder, Andy bred some pretty hot storms, which took him as much by surprise as a thunderstorm that brews up out of a gentle summer day. Lately the slightest frustration might rouse a tumult of anger, even the maddening way Pussel had of asking to be let in and then hesitating while Andy held the door open until she had sniffed every inch of the sill. "Come on, you beast!" he shouted at her, and Pussel hissed at him and made a fat tail as she finally came in.

The climax of this difficult time happened one morning when an unexpected visitor, the person from Porlock, ap-peared out of the blue. Andy had managed to spill the coffee grounds on the floor, Pussel had thrown up her breakfast, and he had gone to the door with an inward groan, fearing the worst.

It was the worst—a youngish matron with beautifully waved and curled gray hair and an artful smile who seemed assured that she could not fail to be welcome.

"Oh, Mr. Lightfoot . . . of course it's you!"

Andy gave her a hunted look and stood there, taking in her bright red suit, several inches above the knee, her silver lipstick, her artificial eyelashes, and, above all, her harsh nasal voice.

"Am I interrupting? I was afraid I might be, but I am just passing through on my way to Nova Scotia, so it had to be now. May I come in?" And she brushed past Andy still talking.

"I'll only stay five minutes," she announced, looking avidly about her. "Why, it's as neat as a pin! I always thought poets lived in chaos . . . and you do it all yourself? No one at all to wash the dishes?" she asked as if speaking to a feeble-minded child.

Andy watched her warily—he felt as if a wild animal had broken into his house without warning. Now she plumped herself down in the armchair by the fire and contemplated him with evident delight.

"I just adore your verse, especially the last book. We need you in this sorry old world. You're a lighthouse, that's what you are. You cast such a strong beam through the night!"

Andy ran a finger along his collar and realized that he was in a sweat. And quite suddenly he felt the anger rising through his chest and up into his throat in a dark flood.

"Who are you?" he asked in a cold voice.

He was now standing behind his desk, at bay.

"You don't know me?" She flung her arms wide in mock

dismay. "Everyone knows *me!* I'm Clara Winkle on the *Early Morning Show*." And she laughed a theatrical laugh meant to be musical. "You funny man, you mean you don't recognize me?"

"Never heard of you. Sorry."

"You don't look at TV?"

"I look at the News at half-past six, and sometimes listen to a concert, or to Thalassa Cruso on Channel Two. But in the morning ... well, I have to work, you know. I have to start the day uncluttered."

"Isn't that sweet? How restful to be anonymous. Just call me 'Angel of the Morning,'" she said with a wink.

It was the first line of a popular song, but of course Andy had no way of knowing that.

"Angel of the morning," she sang loudly and off key. "My rating is almost as high as the *Today Show*, I'll have you know," and now she was flushed. His total indifference had penetrated at last. "You certainly live in a backwater, Mr. Lightfoot. Why, I'm offered thousands by people like you to put them on ... one appearance is worth a full-page ad in the *Times*, I'll have you know."

"Go away, please," Andy said as gently as he could. "I'm tired."

"Try Geritol, it's sure fire," she beamed back.

Andy realized with horror that because he had given her this tiny lien on his state of mind, she was about to move in, armed with patent medicines, psychoanalysts, hot pads, air-conditioners—the works. The adorable image of cool and distinguished Miss Hornbeam floated before his eyes. Why did he have to bear with this invasion, this woman

[41

who represented everything he loathed, when he had waited so many years for Miss Hornbeam to come, with a daisy in her hand, to go for a silent walk through the woods at his side?

Adrenalin shot through him. He was suddenly in a towering rage.

"You have come here uninvited, bringing with you the smell of success, of advertising, of every false value that I have eliminated from my life . . . you pushed your way in and hurled your slick world at me as if it were a horrible Christmas present which, as they say, 'cost plenty' . . . I don't want it! I can't stand it, Miss . . . Mrs. . . . ," he said, having noted the wedding ring on her hand as she fumbled for a cigarette.

"Oh," she breathed in an ecstasy. "Come on the show! Do it on the air. We love to be attacked . . . the audience eats it up. You owe it to yourself, Mr. Lightfoot! Hundreds of people will buy your book."

Andy groaned. You might as well beat your hand on a brass bowl. Help, he cried inwardly, and, for once, Pussel seemed to have been listening, for she came in from the bedroom, where she had been having her morning snooze, took one look at Clara Winkle, and made a fat tail.

The effect of this apparition was instantaneous. Mrs. Winkle's tone changed to that of a maudlin mother.

"Ooh," she crooned, "the pussum-wussum, the itsa-bitsa tiger baby. Come to Momma, you precious lamby."

Pussel advanced, her tail twice its usual size, and gave a quick lash with one paw at the outstretched hand.

"Oh no! She scratched me. Take her away!" Mrs. Winkle

was on her feet and hurrying toward the door. She gave Andy an outraged look. "I've been treated abominably here!" She looked down at her finger which was bleeding. "You and your horrible cat, goodbye!" She slammed the door behind her, dashed for the Jaguar, and shot away before Andy could reach her with an apology or a band-aid.

Pussel meanwhile had settled down complacently, her paws tucked in, on a patch of sunlight on the floor. Everything was calm and intimate again. But what an extraordinary thing! How sudden, how awful it had been! Andy sank down into the old padded chair behind his desk and put his head in his hands—the relief was immense. But in its wake came remorse. It was not Clara Winkle's fault that she was as she was. She had come full of good will. After all she had called him a lighthouse, though he suspected that she had not read the book—there I go again, he scolded himself. I'm being a dreadful snob.

"Pussel," he said severely, "we both behaved rather badly."

But Pussel only looked at him sceptically from her round golden eyes and would admit nothing.

"You're at peace with yourself, are you? Well, I am not," said Andy.

He was thoroughly disgusted by the angry, frustrated baby who had seemed lately to be taking him over. He felt poisoned by rage—senseless rage—and went out and chopped down a lot of small trees and brush behind the barn. At least he could bring some order out of chaos out there, even if he could do little about the chaos inside

[43

himself. But he did feel more composed when he came in two hours later for a glass of milk and a peanut-butter sandwich before his usual afternoon nap.

A light knock woke him out of a doze and he went gladly to open the door to Katy, relieved that the storm had passed and he could feel glad to see someone. Katy was paying her usual holiday visit to her grandparents over the Fourth.

"Hello," he said, looking down at her. "What's on your mind?"

"Salamanders. Gram said I could go catch one if you would go with me down to the woods. Will you?" she asked without stopping for breath.

"Well," Andy considered. Salamanders had not figured in his plans for the afternoon, but, chastened by his rudeness to Mrs. Winkle, he had no choice it seemed. He considered Katy in her new incarnation after a winter away. "You've grown a bit, haven't you?"

The blue jeans climbed halfway up her legs, and she wore her shining fair hair in a pony tail. She had lost two front teeth, and now wore glasses. Katy was seven and a half, she informed him.

"I'm growing up."

"You're a lucky person. I have an idea that I've been growing down."

"How far down?"

"Almost to the floor, almost to the cradle, and I am in need of some strong medicine to start me growing up again. Perhaps," he said, getting out his battered sneakers from the cupboard, "perhaps a salamander might do the trick."

He put them on, standing with one foot on a chair because stooping was harder than it used to be. He fetched a glass jar with a lid from the kitchen shelf and a little basket from the hall, just in case they found moss he could use for his Japanese garden, and he took his big jackknife and a trowel.

"There," he said, "we're ready, I guess, for the expedition."

"Why have you been growing down?" Katy asked as they walked across the meadow toward the woods.

"I have a very recalcitrant, in fact impossible, Muse, Katy."

"What's that? An animal?"

"In a way, yes."

"What sort of animal?"

"A magic animal who helps a poet find his poems."

"With its paws or with its nose?"

"Neither," Andy said, and he could not help laughing, for the image called up a truffle-hunting pig. He laughed so much he had to sit down on a rock, and while he sat there, one arm around Katy, who was giggling because she had evidently made a joke but wasn't quite sure what it was, a ladybird landed on his arm, and together they watched it slowly walking up his leather jacket. "Perhaps she is rather like a ladybird," he sighed, "but not really. She is more like a unicorn."

"Why is she whatever that word was—recal . . . that word you said just now?"

"Because she is busy and has no time to bother with

me."

"Grownups are all like that," Katy said bitterly. "They are all too busy."

"I'm grown up," Andy said, "more or less, anyway. And I have time."

"Oh, well." Katy tossed her pony tail. "You're different. You don't do anything. You don't go to an office."

"No," Andy sighed.

The sigh came from his knowing that most people, even children, thought of him as someone who did nothing. It was rather a lonely business being a poet. No one really knew what it cost, nor, in fact, what it was all about. And sometimes he did not know himself. He felt old and empty.

"Come on." Katy tugged at his sleeve. "I have to be back for cambric tea. Gram's making brownies."

"Oh, very well."

Andy got clumsily to his feet and watched her run ahead through the tall grasses, as tireless and wayward as a butterfly, while he lumbered after her, carrying the huge invisible burden of being himself, an old poet with an impossible Muse.

He could not shake off the mood, even when they did find several efts—vermilion, perfect, tiny creatures, and some extra-good pale-green fat cushions of moss to take home.

Today it all required effort, an effort to be patient, an effort to respond to little Katy, so charming, so sure of her charm, and so very very young. Everything had gone stale for Andy, and the prospect of living another twenty or thirty years without a Muse and in this loathsome condition chilled him to the bone.

For the poet himself is his instrument, and when the instrument gets clouded over, confined, filled with silt and dust, it is a serious matter. Andy had no heart, after all, to remake the Japanese garden. He sat down in the armchair at the cold hearth and smelled the dank smell of his dead pipe, but he had no wish to light it. He had reached a dead end.

Stefan Martin

Two Cripples

CHAPTER 4

There was worse just ahead.

For next day his practical cousin, Hetty, was due to arrive overnight, and she was sure to needle him—she always did. She was ten years older than he and very bossy, for she still thought of him as an invalid incapable of looking after himself. Hetty, Andy had to admit, was absolute Good if Good has no doubts and is concerned only with practical matters. Just as she had nursed him years ago when he had t.b. now she mended his shirts, scrubbed the bathroom floor, and rearranged the cupboards so he could never find a thing after she left, and, of course, she larded these good works with good advice on every possible subject. But she had no more idea of what made him tick than he had of what made Miss Hornbeam tick. And just now Andy was in sore need of understanding.

Hetty was incapable of sitting still without some work in hand, so when they sat down by the fire for a drink before supper, she had a polishing rag in one hand, a copper jug in the other, and a bottle of Noxon at her feet.

"Please be quiet for a moment, Hetty," Andy begged. "Let's talk. You haven't stopped to draw breath. How are things at the library?"

Hetty was librarian in a small town near Boston, and always brought a store of amusing stories to tell him—a safe area for what she imagined to be conversation.

"Oh, very well," she said, taking up her glass and laying down jug and rag. "Cheers!" Then she put the glass down. "What is this stuff?"

"It's not very good, is it?" Andy admitted. "But it's cheap."

"I thought so. Why not open that bottle of J. & B. I brought you?"

So it went. Andy poured her drink down the drain, regretting every drop, opened her bottle, and made her a new one.

"Now can we have a few moments of peace and quiet?"

"Well, don't be so huffy. You're getting queer and irascible, Andy. You really must watch yourself. Old people shouldn't live alone."

"When I go out reading poems, I see hundreds of people. I feel gutted when I get back. I *need* to be alone. Besides, you have no idea what lives pour into this house, the endless letters . . ."

Hetty took a long swallow of her drink and looked at

him tenderly, for under her brusqueries there was real concern.

"You seem rather gloomy, dear. What is the matter? Has your publisher turned down your last book?"

"Good heavens, no! Why should he? My last book did very well indeed as a matter of fact . . . you *know* that!"

"Well . . . when did you last see an M.D.? Can't afford to wait too long."

"Now tell me to take Geritol!" Andy roared. "Good God, Hetty, how obtuse can you be?"

"You may very well be anemic," she continued relentlessly. "Old people often are."

"I'm not an old person yet. I'm not even sixty." Andy took out his pipe to calm his nerves. "I will not be classified and pigeonholed." He tapped some tobacco in firmly, then laid the pipe down to remark, "I'm depressed, that's all." But as he picked it up and lit it, he knew that he should never have admitted depression. Hetty would have the truth now, willy-nilly.

"It's not just that I can't write poems any more. I'm stuck." And he spoke dismally of Miss Hornbeam, of the long, frustrating hopes, and of her lately having bade him cease and desist.

"Good heavens, that pig in a poke! Andy Lightfoot, you are more of a fool than even I can believe. Whatever made you think for an instant that wild-goose chase could lead to anything except disaster? Why should that busy woman have time for you, anyway? She must have thought you were plumb crazy!"

"I don't care what she thinks. I care about what I feel,"

Andy said crossly.

"You live in a world of your own, and if you do that you have to take the consequences."

Hetty was flushed with dismay and, yes — shame. It was quite unbearable that her cousin should make a fool of himself in public. What would people think?

"People will think you're crazy!"

"Maybe I am. But the poems are not. The proof is that they win friends and influence people."

Andy, pleased by this answer, chuckled after it had popped out.

Hetty, reassured by the change of tone, withdrew into a silence to think things over. Andy relit his pipe, which had gone out, and sucked on it. It tasted quite good for a change.

"The point is," she said gently, "that there is something absurd about the situation you have got yourself into. You are an important literary figure, my boy. Isn't it just a little undignified to be so obsessed by a will-o'-the-wisp who made it clear some time ago that she was not interested and could not help you?"

"You see, Hetty dear, this is a matter of poetry, not of dignity."

"I don't understand you at all," she said sadly.

Would it do any good to try to explain? Andy was touched by her change of mood. The bossy old cousin had faded away. He sensed that she felt helpless, left out.

"Let's have another drink," Andy said, and went off with the glasses.

"The thing is," he said as he handed her her glass and

sat down again, "that you look at poetry as if it were carpentry. In some ways, that is just what it is—at least after
a poem is on the table, so to speak. But one has very little
control over what gets the poem on the table, and that's
the hell of it. God knows I didn't choose Miss Hornbeam.
These are not affairs in which reason can operate, Hetty,
and that is why they are so baffling."

For months Andy had longed to talk to someone, anyone, and for once Hetty had softened enough from her
rigid stance to be able to listen. He was grateful, and he
tried to explain.

"I suppose that is why Plato would not have allowed
poets into his Republic. They are, inevitably, disturbed
and disturbing people, vulnerable, anarchic, never quite
grown up, feeling their way by hunches, in touch at times
with mysterious powers, always engaged in knocking walls
down, opening locked doors, and making nuisances of
themselves." Andy suddenly put his head in his hands and
groaned. "I'm just so damned angry all the time, Hetty, it
scares me."

For once Hetty was silent.

"I haven't written a poem for months."

"I'm sorry, dear. I wish I could help but . . ."—she steeled
herself to say it now—"you simply have to get over this
Muse, as you call her, and try to find another."

"One doesn't *find* a Muse," he said bitterly. "They come
. . . and they don't come often to dotty old poets, I can
tell you."

"Perhaps you could take a little trip . . . go to Greece . . ."
But this suggestion received only an ironic smile.

"*Nous avons bâti sur le sable des cathédrales périssables*," he murmured, walking up and down. "I was a whole shining person, full of gifts, during two long years of silence. That is what is so hard. The silence was *alive*, Hetty, I know it was! I just can't accept that when so little was needed, so very little—it didn't cost her anything—Miss Hornbeam should refuse to give it."

He turned to Hetty now with passionate conviction, for once lit up, his real self in her presence, and the intensity of his being, an old man with the fresh ring of a boy in his voice, touched her in regions where she was usually too shy to enter.

"Feeling asks feeling, Andy. A person in Miss Hornbeam's position has learned that she cannot afford it, I expect."

"Then she's a cripple!"

"Oh, Andy, we all are!" The words were wrenched out of Hetty because she envied him this capacity for intense feeling. It was something, she realized, that she would never experience, could know nothing about. "Some people might say that an old man who never married, who lives alone and writes poems, is a cripple, too. But your innocence, dear Andy, your vulnerability, your caring so much too much, all that makes you the poet you are, is your *strength*. Maybe what makes Miss Hornbeam a cripple is *her* strength, can't you see?"

"And as cripples, we cripple each other," he said sharply. "What a grim little story it turns out to be."

Andy banged his fist down on the table, but, for once, something stopped the anger. He went into the kitchen and set himself to cooking their dinner, and he was thinking about Hetty as he laid the steak under the broiler and put on water for the peas, and how good it is to have some family, someone who has to accept one as one is. It had, after all, been a great relief to talk so openly, and at least this time he had managed not to go off like a clumsy firecracker into one of his shameful tantrums.

When he came back to set the table, Hetty was rubbing the copper pot till it shone like flame itself in the firelight, and the silence between them, a silence after real talk, felt good.

Andy Has an Inspiration

CHAPTER 5

After Hetty left the next morning and that other silence fell, not the silence of companionship but the silence of solitude, Andy wandered about sharpening pencils in a complete funk. On his desk lay the muddled version of a translation he had been working on for days. On the mantel the copper jug Hetty had polished so industriously gleamed at him, and he picked it up and held it for a moment. As usual she had swept out the cobwebs and left a challenge behind her. I simply cannot bear this joyless existence another day, he thought. I have to invent *something!*

What kind of new experience or challenge could he feed his depression? For that, surely, was what was needed. No more brooding, but action. Something he could get his mind on, another track . . . yes . . . he took a book on mushrooms down from the shelves. Hetty had given it to him years before because she hoped he would learn to distinguish the eatable ones. What about a thorough study of mushrooms? But mushrooms came in September, not in late June and July, and he really could not wait another day. What if he learned Russian—then he could read Tchekov in the original—or what if he built a kiln and became a potter? But none of these ideas felt real somehow. They lay there in his consciousness like infertile seeds.

Andy opened the back door for Pussel, who had been sitting silently in front of it for some time as if it were a mouse hole. She shook one paw, went slowly out as if the world were one big hazard, and then suddenly flew off and raced up a tree. The sun was out for a change, and Andy followed her into the garden in quiet desperation. It was an irresistible gardening day, with the earth so damp and the weeds so thick and easy to pull, and pretty soon he was whistling in spite of himself.

An hour later, feeling a bit stiff in the knees from so much stooping, he remembered that he must have somewhere a weeder with a long handle, and went into the barn to look for it. The old horse stall there had become a general dump for flowerpots, discarded tools, a clumsy hand-mower, the storm windows, and various other accumulations. Andy was puttering about among them, when he suddenly noticed the iron ring fastened to the back wall. He pushed a pile of seedling boxes aside and found himself standing where the old horse once had stood, looking out into the barn through a small opening . . . and then it came to him, in the very instant when he noticed that the horse had chewed off a depression just right for leaning a chin on, that the new thing he would learn was donkey. Donkey, of course! The barn needed a donkey in that stall, and he needed a donkey.

Like all ideas of genius, once it had swum into his ken it seemed perfectly obvious. Here was the stall. Outside was a meadow. And the Crockers up the road had a beautiful donkey called Whiffenpoof. Andy had wondered about her often—whether they had time to take her out as often as she would have liked, for all winter she stood there in a small shed with several calves, an old sheep, and two goats. The thought had been "donkey" rather than "horse" because, Andy realized, Whiffenpoof had been in the back of his mind for a long time. But would the Crockers be willing to lend her for the summer?

His mind was racing ahead now. It would mean fencing in part of the meadow and this problem loomed rather large. Andy spent the rest of the morning pacing off and measuring what seemed an ample space of green, he called the Grain and Feed Store, and made various additions and subtractions on an old pad. It would be expensive, he had to admit, but after all a man with such a life-enhancing idea in his head does not pinch pennies—and he could do the work himself with just some help from the Crockers, surely.

The big question remained whether they would be willing to lend the precious animal. They were poor, but they were also rich, for they had adopted innumerable animals of all kinds, and life on the farm was an endless series of adventures, of births and deaths, of escapes and chases, and of new investments in joy, such as Muscovy ducks or large white rabbits with black-velvet ears and noses. They loved their animals as members of the family and might hesitate to let Whiffenpoof out of their sight, even for a few months.

What with their muddy road and his depression, Andy had not been up to see the Crockers all spring. Now he put on a clean red shirt, and managed to get the old Chevy started after some tinkering with the spark plugs (the damp weather had subdued them), and off he went, up and down the steep dirt road that led from the village to the distant hill where the Crockers' farm stood above a fine pond. It was small, dilapidated, and hugged the earth, but it had many extensions in the shape of sheds and barns, a large vegetable garden at its back, and a small fenced-in flower garden in front where Mary grew the best sweet peas for miles around. It was a homey place, even to the abandoned cars put out to pasture here and there, the rabbit hutches in a row to the left, and always a goose or a duck or a bobtailed cat asleep under the hay wagon.

If someone had asked Andy, "What is the place where life is richest around here?" he would have answered, "The Crockers', of course."

They were a close-knit clan, held together by a frail-looking woman, Meg Crocker, working together like a small cooperative, absorbing children who had built houses in the valley below the homestead, and grandchildren, who poured in and out of Meg's all day long. Open the door and you found yourself in a tiny kitchen bursting with life, from the basket of kittens under the stove to the old dog under the table, a canary in a cage at the window, a crock of parsley on one sill and geraniums crowding their way toward the light on the other. Someone was sure to be cooking a meal, while someone else sat nursing a baby. One cold midwinter morning Andy had found Mary cooking pancakes for Whiffenpoof.

As the Chevy panted up the last steep hill, greeted by loud barkings and the cries of a flock of children, Andy thought of those pancakes with a qualm. They were the visible sign of the affection in which Whiffenpoof was held. How could her family bear to part with her? How could he ask? But then he remembered Meg on the phone one bleak March morning, how he had explained that he was so low in his mind he couldn't work, and how she had comforted him. "It will come out all right, Andy. Just be patient."

She knew what it was to sow a whole field and then have a late frost kill the young shoots, and she knew what it was to have an animal die for no apparent reason, just like a poem. Andy's spirits rose as he saw the blue flags in flower by the pond and the Muscovy ducks down there, for he felt that somehow or other Meg would understand that Whiffenpoof was an absolute necessity for his peace of mind.

This late in the morning the family was out in the big field hoeing and weeding the long rows of corn, potatoes, beans, and squash—all except Miggy, Meg's granddaughter, who ran out of the barn to greet Andy, and Mary, who was no doubt in the kitchen cooking their midday meal.

"We have two new calves," Miggy called out. "Come and see!"

Was there ever a time when there was no newborn creature to rejoice in at the Crockers'? Andy went gladly into the barn with its good animal smell, ammonia and the sweet breath of cows and hay. He rubbed the white star on the black calf's forehead, and admired the tiny buff-colored one with her dark deer eyes, still rather tottery, so she was lying down.

"I have come about Whiffenpoof," he said solemnly.

"What about her?" Miggy asked, wondering what on earth Whiffenpoof had done, since she was standing quietly in her stall. "She's O.K."

"I know."

Miggy, mystified, followed Andy's long purposeful stride toward the shed where Whiffenpoof lived—a shed hardly as big as the room of a tiny house.

"Where's everyone else?"

The place was empty except for the lank, gray, long-eared presence standing patiently in the far corner, face to the wall.

"The pony's grazing. So are the goats. And we sold the two other calves last week."

For Andy it was a grave moment, for he was looking at Whiffenpoof in an entirely new light. She had become for him, in the last hours, a mythical beast, the incarnation of hope. For once he did not even go and stroke her nose. He stood and gazed as if in a dream. And Miggy, beside him, wondered whatever could be on his mind.

"Doesn't she ever get out to graze?"

"Well, she's awful lame, Andy. I do take her out when I can get her to go—but we're busy these days, with the garden and all, and it's been so damp too. It makes her ankles swell."

"Come," said Andy firmly. "I have something to ask you and your grandmother."

Until this moment he had thought of Whiffenpoof only in terms of his own need. Now the marvelous thought came to him that perhaps the need was mutual. Those ankles . . . that limp . . . they gave him courage.

So they walked on past a hutch where he could hear the guinea hens chattering their alarm at the approach of a stranger, and past the horse barn, out under the old apple tree standing in a snow of fallen petals, through the gate and into the field. The family waved as he approached —Martin, the eldest, who was the real farmer, his sister Jane, and Meg herself, glad to stand a minute, no doubt, after the long stooping.

"Well, Andy! Haven't seen you for ages!" Meg's welcoming smile enfolded him. "How are things down there? Slugs eating the garden up?"

"A terrible spring, terrible," Andy said, "nothing but weeds to show . . . and besides that, I'm in a funk. Can't work. Can't manage a line."

"We're all behind this year."

How could he ever put his question? Andy stood there, lost in doubts suddenly, looking at his muddy feet, feeling the barriers of reality set up against his wild dream.

"You look peaked. That flu hangs on, don't it?" Meg pulled back a wisp of hair and surveyed him as if he were a plant that needed sun and water.

"I thought perhaps I might borrow Whiffenpoof for the summer."

He had taken the plunge. Now he waited. Meg and Miggy exchanged a quick glance.

"I'll fence in half the big meadow for her," he said quickly, to remove any doubt they might be feeling. "She can sleep in my barn. I have a big stall there all ready for her."

"Well,"—Martin rubbed his chin—"we'd have to get her down."

"I know," Andy nodded, realizing what a harebrained scheme it was after all.

"She's so stiff in her ankles she could never make it on foot," Miggy said.

They all looked at him now, trying to read his face. He sensed their bewilderment, but how could he possibly explain?

"It sounds foolish, but . . . well, it came to me this morning that if Whiffenpoof were out there in the meadow, I'd feel better. I might be able to work."

He didn't lift his head, but he knew they were exchanging silent messages and that a decision was being sensed out among them, as in a Quaker meeting.

"Lately," he said, in a last effort, "everything has gone stale in me and around me. I don't know what to do with myself."

He was a beggar before them in their perfect innocence. But now he managed a smile, and it helped, for he saw their faces concerned, alert, really listening.

"I need to learn something new. I thought learning donkey might be just what I need."

Of course his work was as mysterious to the Crockers as theirs often was to him. And now they all laughed with the kindliest amusement and pleasure at the thought that a donkey might help a poet write poems. An invisible assent passed between Martin, Jane, Miggy, and Meg. Then Meg spoke for them all.

"We'd be glad to help."

Martin nodded.

"Miggy and I will bring Whiffenpoof down in the truck when you're ready for her."

Whew! Relief made Andy turn pink. And before he left, Miggy had agreed to come down with her mother, Olive, and Mary, and help him put up the fence some night after supper. On an impulse, he asked whether he might not borrow one of the goats as well, "so that Whiffenpoof won't be lonely."

"The goats are old," Miggy said, "and they have never been away from home."

Andy saw that she could not be asked to part with so many treasures for a whole summer, so he let that thought drop.

Before he left, he went into Whiffenpoof's stall and stroked her long ears, so thickly furred inside, and felt a magic thrill in his fingers, because she had already become a sacred animal, and he sensed that he would have a great deal to learn from her.

Kingdom Come

CHAPTER 6

For the next days, Andy forgot all about his desk, while he prepared for the adventure of Whiffenpoof. Stakes and huge rolls of wire four feet high were dumped in the field one morning and he had a splendid time driving the stakes in. But then there was the question of a gate and gateposts.

Dear me, Andy thought, for carpentry was not really his thing. He could putter around with a hammer and nails but he hadn't the foggiest idea how to make a gate, and besides he had lent his really good saw to someone years ago and forgotten to ask for it back. He considered this problem while he cleared out the piles of flowerpots and gardening things that had accumulated in the stall, among them a splendid shovel for shoveling manure. When everything was shipshape, Andy stood where Whiffenpoof would stand and peered out as she would soon be doing. It felt quite snug and homey.

In the dusky recesses of the barn, his eye lighted on a long square beam that would make splendid gateposts if he could lay his hands on a saw. Oh yes, the barn was coming alive . . . it had been empty far too long. True, the Crockers stored hay from his meadow there all winter till the lean March days when they began to run out of fodder, and that sweet smell of hay provided a nostalgic whiff of summer when it got down to thirty below. And true, the old harness still hung on the back wall, gathering dust, just as he had found it when he first moved in years ago. But old harness and hay do not do what the stamp of hoofs at night and the breathing of a living animal would do to make the barn a real barn again, not just a receptacle of nostalgias and dreams.

And I, Andy thought,—I too will become real again and cease to be an empty shell, or so he hoped it might be, although of course he could not be sure. It might all turn out pure folly and leave him worse off and considerably poorer in every way than he had been before. But nothing risk, nothing have, Andy hummed as he struggled with the huge beam.

Michael Hunter saw him trying to drag it out.

"That's rather a heavy load for one man, isn't it?"

He came swiftly to the rescue and together they laid it down in the field.

"Yes," Andy puffed, for he was badly out of breath, "lucky you came along."

Michael did odd jobs when he felt like it, between going

to high school and fishing, and now before he was aware what he had got himself in for he had agreed to make the gate, saw the beam, and drive in the posts. It was an expensive deal, Andy thought, but Michael evidently needed cash. He was in love, and that meant not only having money to spend on his girl but also investments in studded belts and cowboy shirts and all sorts of gear to prove what a handsome fellow he was. Anyway Michael agreed to have the gate set up within five days. And what's more he kept his word.

The swinging gate and sturdy posts gave the meadow a purposeful look it had never had before, and Andy smiled to think that a single donkey was transforming him into a gentleman farmer.

So far so good, though he did feel a little anxious still about the actual fencing. But Miggy, Olive, and Mary Crocker came down after their supper one warm evening —when the black flies were at their worst—and they all set to work. The roll of wire was too heavy for any one person to lift and was clumsy to handle when they did get it upright. The hammer kept getting lost in the grass. The black flies made every move just a little harder than it needed to be, as hands flew up to slap and ward off the silent deadly throngs around eyes and on the backs of necks and ankles. Andy found his vocabulary of swear words in several languages very useful, but the Crockers, he noticed, met all the irritations with unfailing good humor—they just kept at it, clumsy often but always determined. Even so, they would never have finished that night unless Tom Evans had happened by, taken in the situation, and rushed in with the vigor of a battalion to help win what surely would have been a losing battle without his help. By the time the last few feet of wire were hammered into posts, they could hardly see, and even the indomitable Crockers were too done in to stay for a coke. And after promising to bring Whiffenpoof down the following Wednesday, they chugged off homewards in the dark. Tom drank down a beer in one long gulp and hurried home to supper. Alone again, Andy sank into his armchair absurdly tired, and absurdly happy. It did not occur to him that the thought of Miss Hornbeam had not crossed his mind all day.

He woke on Wednesday morning with his heart full of tremor and anticipation, but in that instant between sleep and waking he could not remember what it was that was about to take place. Was he—childhood dream—pitching for the Red Sox? Was he in the middle of a great joyful poem calling him imperiously to his desk? Or was he about to set out alone to sail round the world? Then he remembered—of course, this was Whiffenpoof's day, so long awaited, so passionately hoped for! He leapt out of bed, leaving those dreams of glory behind him, and went to the window to see what kind of weather God was providing this morning for an old poet and a donkey. Alas, there was an overcast sky; dark clouds were piling down from the north where the storms came from. He went to the door and opened it and tasted hot, moist air. Oh dear, the black flies! Well, there was nothing to do but wait and hope. He at least was fully prepared for the adventure.

There were large supplies of carrots in the frigidaire and a box of lump sugar on the shelf. Out by the splendid gate he had placed a blue plastic pail with a mixture of anti-fly goozelum in it, and a large sponge beside it. And in the barn forty pounds of oats stood in paper bags.

The first thing Andy did when he had shaved and dressed was to run out to the barn. The stall looked a little like an apartment just before a tenant moves in, rather too clean, a little desolate somehow. But he was pleased to see that the sticky roll of flypaper had already begun to function. This had been a final inspiration, and he had driven into town only yesterday to get one and hang it near Whiffenpoof's tail but not near enough for her to get entangled in it. (Andy had dreadful memories of a Laocoön struggle with just such a thing as a child.) Still and all, the barn was not, he supposed, the really important thing. Surely Whiffenpoof, after her long winter in prison, would be happy out under open sky and on soft turf most of the time, and her stall would be more a shelter in time of need than a real home. Andy gazed anxiously up at the threatening sky. The immensity of taking on a strange animal whose ways and needs he could only dimly imagine weighed like the atmosphere itself.

I am an absurd person, he thought, but he felt no shame, for the absurdity of borrowing Whiffenpoof was the right kind, his own special kind, a secret madness that the world could accept . . . and in this respect it was a far better lunacy than his capture by the recalcitrant and far too public Miss Hornbeam, for that was a lunacy the world would never condone or understand. It had set him apart in an anguished dialogue with God. He was pacing up and down now in a mood of extreme clarity, as often happens when one is waiting for something long expected to happen. Whiffenpoof, he imagined, would bring him back from those high desolate places, to the good simple things of earth . . . but would he ever feel joy again? Would wrath and gloom (cardinal sins, he knew) ever leave his heart, he wondered.

Where were the Crockers anyway? Andy felt suddenly wildly impatient, and shaken too by all the doubts he had kept at bay while there was so much to do to make ready. What if it proved to be all a crazy mistake—time-consuming and, in some unknown way, only baffling to the hungry, loving boy buried somewhere in the cross old poet?

Finally he heard the ancient Crocker truck wheezing and snorting its way through the village, and there it was, and there beside Miggy, who was standing in the back, were two long ears. Whiffenpoof's head was out of sight behind the truck cabin.

"Kingdom come," Andy breathed as he ran out to help. Martin had backed the truck against the steep bank across the road, with the idea, no doubt, that when he let the back down, Whiffenpoof could walk right out like a princess. But none of them had reckoned with her lameness. Whiffenpoof was reluctant to move at all. Only little by little was she persuaded to back out, one step at a time, and, with the help of Miggy's pushing and tugging, to scramble down the bank, where she stood, ears back, in the middle of the road.

After looking both ways along the road to be sure that

no car was coming, Andy took one side of the halter while Miggy still held onto the other, and together they dragged Whiffenpoof, step by step, toward the meadow and into the enclosure, where they fastened the new gate firmly behind her.

"There you are!" Miggy beamed at Andy, but he was not looking at Miggy. He was entirely concentrated on the huge gray head, the dark eyes sheltered by eyelashes worthy of Greta Garbo, and the heavenly ears. He leaned over and silently stroked the gray-velvet nose, then took a lump of sugar out of his pocket. Soft lips picked it up from the palm of his hand and he heard a satisfying crunch as it was savored.

Only then did he lift his head and answer Miggy's smile. "Why is she so lame, Miggy?"

"They think it's arthritis—but maybe the hoofs could be cleaned out and that might help."

Andy took down a man's name to phone about this, and then, before he quite knew what was happening, the Crockers had come and gone like jinn and he was alone with Whiffenpoof. But he could not stay. Like all poets, who must constantly examine experience, he could hardly wait to get away and think about her. He sat down at his desk, lit his pipe, and considered her—her great and terrifying size (for she looked to him almost as big as a horse), the softness of her large dark eyes, above all the long furry ears that were hardly ever still, as sensitized as semaphores.

After he had calmed down and puffed away for a few moments, he went to the window. There she was, a donkey in his meadow, already nibbling greedily at the silky rich grass, head down, tail swinging in a steady hypnotic rhythm, back and forth, back and forth, as if she had always been there. It was a peaceful and exhilarating sight.

Already, in just a few minutes of this solitude *à deux*, Andy could feel that the tightrope that had lain slack at his feet for months had become attached to Whiffenpoof. His attention was engaged. He was no longer locked inside himself, and although the new adventure felt rather perilous (for how was he going to get her in and out of the barn on those shaky ankles?), that was part of the charm, and Andy was suffused by a kind of inward smile.

He called the man Miggy had recommended, John Bean, and told him what was needed. Bean was not eager, said he was very busy, but Andy found a new authority in his voice, the voice of a man concerned about an animal, and Mr. Bean finally agreed to come over the next evening. It was a small triumph but it seemed a good augury.

It gave him the courage to go out and try sponging the huge animal off with the anti-fly stuff, for she was now wagging her head as well as her tail, and Andy hurried to unfasten the gate and relieve her as best he could. He started with her neck and the sensitive place between her ears, rubbed down her furry cheeks, and then her breastbone and down the inside of her front legs—so far, so good. She gave him a wary look, but seemed quite willing to be approached in this intimate fashion by her new friend, and for Andy it was a way of really getting to know her, every bone and soft place all over her. But what about the rear end? Would she kick? The legs so elegant and thin, like a deer's, he thought, the hide so tender at the soft hams! He went at it warily, but she stood quite still, turning her head to observe him, making no move. Only when he tried to sponge along her stomach and its thick fringe of fur, her skin twitched, and one back leg came up gently to push him off.

"All right, old thing." He patted her shaggy forehead, feeling that they already knew each other better, and left her to her pleasures.

When he looked out an hour later, she was no longer swinging her tail, and her ears had stopped wagging back and forth. She was munching happily, moving from clover to delicious tufts of sweet grass, and Andy felt the joy it is to give nourishment, a whole meadow, a banquet in fact, to a new friend.

So far she had made no sound.

But the silence was inhabited. While she munched, Andy worked well, so well that he forgot all about Whiffenpoof till nearly one o'clock. Then he came to with a start because he heard rain on the roof.—Good heavens! There she was, standing at the gate swinging her lowered head back and forth in a dreadful compulsive way, as Andy had seen animals do in a zoo. He ran out without stopping for a raincoat, though he did remember to take a carrot with him.

"Dear soul," he murmured, "I had quite forgotten you!"

She lifted her head at his approach, pricked her ears, and for the first time made a sound that might have been a greeting—or might have been a sound of distress; it was hard to tell which was intended for all that came out was a painful wheeze, a subdued, panting, whispered scream.

"Dear me," Andy said, "is it as bad as all that?"

Her ears went flat against her head. Hurrying to unfasten the gate, he stepped in beside her, and, while she
munched her carrot, managed to attach the rope Miggy
had braided for him to the halter.

"All right then, come and see the barn!"

He gave a sharp tug, and she took a few steps, stopped
dead to sniff at a tuft of clover and seize on it. Her genius
is in her nose and lips, Andy realized. This was the highly
sensitized area.

Little by little they reached the gravelly drive. Here she
paused to snuffle the surface, as if she had something on
her mind. But a rousing clap of thunder startled her into
motion again, and, once inside the barn, she followed Andy
docilely into her stall and stood quiet while he tied her up
to the ring.

"O.K., girl?" he asked as he went past her little window
on his way out of the barn.

She gave a kind of snuffle, looked at him gravely, her
ears pricked forward.

By four the storm had blown over and Andy decided he
had better get her out again as she might be hungry. But
this proved to be rather an ordeal. Lumps of sugar, carrots, were absorbed eagerly enough, but Whiffenpoof did
not want to leave the barn. After all, Andy thought, I cannot expect to know everything about this mysterious being
all at once. So he waited and waited and waited, and finally
Whiffenpoof reached the gravel drive of her own free will.
Then he learned why she had snuffled so eagerly on her

way in, for she suddenly folded her front legs and before
Andy quite knew how it had been done, she was rolling
on her back! It had all the humor of the incongruous and
Andy laughed aloud, remembering how he had laughed
in the same way years ago when he had seen a dignified
penguin in his black-and-white tuxedo suddenly lie down
on his stomach and slide down a slide. Whiffenpoof had
so much dignity and the sight of her performing such a
caper was as droll.

All very well, but it was not a happy sight, when he had
finally got her into the meadow, to see that she was again
swinging her head back and forth at the gate in that
strange compulsive gesture, and seemed not at all interested in eating delicious wet grass. Something was the
matter, but what? It turned into an anxious afternoon.
Andy could not settle down to anything. He did a little
gardening, but it was disturbing to do it in the presence
of the monotonous swinging of that head, that whole gray
body in some state of desperation he could not understand. So he took her in early that evening for her supper.
His fears that she would balk proved unfounded; she
pulled him instead of his pulling her, and she bumped the
pail about to get the very last of the oats. When he left
her, she pushed her gray-velvet nose through the little
window and held it there, breathing loudly, until he had
stroked it. It was about the best sensation he had had in
his fingers for a long time.

Of course he had to go back in the dusk to be sure she
was all right. Where are the ears? he thought, peering
through the little window. And then he saw that the ears

were close to the floor. She was lying down, her forelegs in, in much the same way that Pussel and Sneakers folded theirs in when in a state of contentment. He gave a last look at the great bowed head, which had not moved, and walked softly out, and pulled the big barn door shut.

And that is the morning and evening of the first day, he thought as he got into bed, deliciously tired and at peace with himself and the world. Twice in the night he heard the hollow sound of hoof on floorboard as, no doubt, Whiffenpoof got up. Then there was silence. But even through the walls of house and barn, and through his dreamless sleep, Andy was aware of her breathing, and early in the morning he found himself murmuring, still half asleep, "She makes time stand still."

He sat up with the force of this insight, for was it not that, just that suspension of time, that the Muse had made possible? It had to do then with a state of being, with something opened in himself, with some joining of a buried self with primary powers. But he was too sleepy to figure it out, and lay down again, still wondering, and was fast asleep before he knew it.

Learning the Language

CHAPTER 7

For the first time in months there was reason to get up early instead of turning over and trying to put off the gloomy day ahead, and Andy was out of bed before he had really opened his eyes. He did not wait to shave, just pulled on jeans, boots, and an old sweater, and was off to the barn. Already, in the distance, he heard that stifled bray, which he took to be a sign at least of recognition if not of welcome. So Whiffenpoof too was awake in her world.

Andy pushed the big barn door wide.

"Good morning! How's the girl?"

The gray nose pushed its way through the aperture to

be stroked, and eager lips grasped the carrot Andy had remembered to put in his pocket. There was a smell of fresh manure, aromatic and rich, and Andy went to work at once to clean things up, shoveling up the droppings into his weed cart, a neat, easy way, he thought, rather pleased with his invention, to get things out back of the barn. Already he was imagining how the garden would flourish next year when he could spread the rich stuff around. He had not thought of fertilizer as one of the gifts Whiffenpoof would bring, but clearly she was going to make his world flower. He chuckled at the thought of fertilizer and poems, and what a splendid combination they were.

After he had finished cleaning up, Andy went off with the pail to get fresh water, rejoicing in the early morning light, dew shining on the grass, the hills floating on a white band of mist, and the white-throated sparrow repeating his haunting phrase. How long had it been since he had been out early enough to catch it, and all the other sweet pipings and songs, as if every bush had its bird, while the soft air was scissored overhead by swallows' wings?

When he got back with the water, Whiffenpoof was breathing hard, and this, Andy thought, must mean, "Where are my oats, old man?"

"Just a minute, girl," he said. "All in good time."

He was enjoying creating a routine, setting a rhythm to be kept going through all the donkey days, a routine that would frame the timeless world of himself and Whiffenpoof. At any rate she certainly enjoyed her oats and was blowing out words of praise, little snorts, when he went in to make his own breakfast of bacon and eggs and toast and coffee. He hoped Whiffenpoof's had tasted half as good.

Of course she must be waiting now, impatiently, to get out to her green meadow and graze, so Andy went right out again after breakfast without lighting his morning pipe, thinking how good it was to feel the tug of some need other than his own.

But Whiffenpoof was anything but eager. He managed to get her out of her stall and into the barn beside the old Chevy, but there she stopped dead and whiffled around the floor, tasting odd bits of hay left over from last year. There she took her stand and refused to move one step farther into the June morning where the dew was melting on the grass.

"Come *on!*" Andy was suddenly impatient. "Come *on*, Whiffenpoof!"

But her back legs were splayed, her whole body leaning back on them in a determined No. Her ears lay flat and she had a wicked gleam in her eye. Whatever had come to him in the guise of this beast was not going to be as easy as all that. Miss Hornbeam refused to answer, but at least she was mobile and far away. But here he was locked in frustration with a mysterious being who simply stood there, monolithic and stubborn.

"Well, Whiffenpoof, if you can be balky, I can be patient," he said cheerfully, letting the rope he had been tugging at go slack. The Crockers had warned him not to give in to her, ever, or she would become the master. But do I want to master her, he asked himself? No, it is not my wish to master anyone, even a donkey. So let her have her will, he thought, standing quiet, one hand in his pocket, entirely nonchalant.

"We shall just be patient with each other, old thing," he murmured, and caressed the soft tuft of hair between her ears.

What had almost become a bitter and fruitless tug of war subsided into a kind of meditation. Andy stood there. Whiffenpoof stood there. There was no hurry in this timeless world. And it occurred to Andy that there was a kind of peace in waiting—waiting together. For what he did not really know.

That morning an hour floated away into the gentle air before the gate finally closed behind Whiffenpoof in the meadow, and before Andy had washed her down against the flies and could leave her there. But when he finally did go in to his desk, and lit his pipe, the tempo of the day had been subtly changed. He had stood a long time beside a fellow creature, asking nothing, and somehow, during that limbo, he had felt peace—peace, so long absent— well up in him.

Perhaps it was because he had been able to push anger aside, had not allowed it to take possession, for he now understood quite well why a balky donkey arouses the instinct to beat. Well, he said to himself, lifting Sneakers off his manuscript and laying her gently in the armchair, maybe that donkey is going to teach me patience.

But for the moment Whiffenpoof was not much help to the poet. Andy kept going to the window to see how she was getting on. He suddenly remembered that since John Bean was coming that afternoon, he had better ask Miggy to come down, in case they needed her help if the donkey acted up. Andy imagined hoof-cutting for a donkey as rather like going to a dentist for a human being. It could not be a pleasant operation, however much relief might be felt after it was done.

At mid-morning, when he went out with a lump of sugar, he was dismayed to see that, far from liking her meadow, Whiffenpoof was standing at the gate, head bent, in an attitude of dejection. What did she want? To be taken back to her stall? Yet all around her was a delicious mixed meal of tasseled grasses, clover heads and their sweet leaves, daisies, strawberry in flower, even a couple of thistles, and heaven knows what other delicacies, as elegant and various as a Japanese meal. None of it tempted her, it would seem, and as he left her, her ears pricked and she gave him an accusing look, or so he imagined. Of course she might be lonely—lonely for the busy farmyard up at the Crockers', a kind of Times Square of animals and children.

Clearly Whiffenpoof was displacing a great deal of atmosphere already, and it crossed Andy's mind that he might have made a grave mistake and that, far from being a help, the donkey might turn into one more distraction to keep him irritated, dispersed, and unable to work.

But it did not turn into a wasted morning after all. In fact by noon he was deeply immersed, locked in a delightful battle to bring out alive a poem he had abandoned weeks before—a poem about the early spring light when leaves are still transparent, and it is all a gauzy, veiled brilliance, layer on layer of many-colored light, through which he could still see the distant hills, now, in summer, all shut away behind opaque green. It had been a long time since words had come to him fresh, not worn-out counters to be manipulated. Wonderful it was to feel his blood flow faster as he set down an adjective, and a faint sweat gathered on his upper lip. The Japanese have a word for this disengagement that accompanies expertise at the highest level. *Muga* they call it, when dance and dancer become one and all is fused. It had been a long time since Andy had experienced it. Had it come to him now because of a donkey out there in the meadow, a balky donkey, an irritated irritating donkey whom he must come to understand? Close to the absurd, close to the divine, the old man sat at his desk smiling.

But by four in the afternoon, when Andy finally got up, stretched, and thought about eating a little something, Whiffenpoof was in a bad temper. Apparently she had not budged from the gate. She stood there weaving her bowed head back and forth in that compulsive and terrible rhythm of the caged. There was nothing for it but to let her go back to her stall and bring her out again when John Bean arrived at six. This time she did not balk, although the limp seemed rather worse than usual. But somehow Andy felt little connection between them—he had, in the last hours, become her keeper rather than her friend. And she herself remained a mystery. Would she still be a mystery at the end of the summer? Andy's mood about his adventure had gone up and down rather wildly that day.

It was a relief when jovial John Bean drove up in his bright red truck, and when, a moment later, Miggy turned in in a dying black Ford—a relief to be able to ask questions, to talk in human language for a change.

"Why doesn't she like it outdoors? She just begs to get back to her stall. I can't understand it."

"If her ankles hurt, that may be a reason. Let's have a look."

Mr. Bean and Miggy went into the barn and dragged Whiffenpoof out, Mr. Bean pulling and Miggy pushing. And Andy was rather glad to see that they did not have an easy time of it.

"Uh-huh," Mr. Bean nodded, "she's arthritic all right. See that swelling?" and he pointed to the thickened bone at the ankle.

Miggy stood at the donkey's head, holding it hard against her breast, her own legs strongly braced and wide apart. Like all gestures to do with work, and especially to do with work with animals, it had beauty, and Andy looked hard at Miggy with Whiffenpoof because a poem was swimming into his ken. Mr. Bean, in a leather apron, with a small, sharp, curved knife in his hand, was ready now to begin the operation. It was clever the way he lifted one foreleg, bending it at the knee and resting the hoof in the palm of his left hand while right hand and knife went to work.

"Time she was relieved of some of that," he said, slicing off thin slices, horny half-moons, with quick, precise cuts of the knife. "You'll see, she'll walk better after this."

But just then he hit a tender spot and Whiffenpoof wheeled sharply and broke away.

"Now, now, quiet . . ."

Andy ran in to get a lump of sugar, and when he got

back Mr. Bean had started on the other front hoof. It was fascinating to watch the man at work, fascinating as it always is to watch skill and knowledge at play to relieve suffering. Andy was silent, suffering with Whiffenpoof. Twice she flung both Miggy and John Bean off and showed the whites of her eyes as she tossed her head, but after a lump of sugar and some firm quiet words from Mr. Bean, she seemed to accept that this time there was no way out. At last all four hoofs had been trimmed and the grass littered with tiny white half-moons.

"There, now she may even *ask* to go out to the meadow," Mr. Bean said, wiping his hands on his leather apron.

"About the arthritis," Andy asked anxiously, "can anything be done?"

"No harm in getting a vet over."

"I wonder why she's so balky." Andy felt that he must get all the help he could before being abandoned with this foreigner whose language he had not begun to master.

"They all are," Miggy said, smiling at him and his anxiety. "Don't worry. Just give her a little tap with a stick when she balks."

Easier said than done, Andy thought, when I am pulling her forward by the rope and can't possibly reach her behind.

He gave Mr. Bean ten dollars. No wonder the Crockers did not often have the hoofs trimmed! Ten dollars was a lot of money. But Andy had accepted long ago, when it came to fencing and the gate, that Whiffenpoof was a pure extravagance, as expensive as several cases of champagne. She was a calculated risk. Andy savored this businesslike way of disposing of the matter.

As the days wore on, Whiffenpoof grew balkier every morning. Andy felt troubled. Something was missing; some mysterious accord between them had still not come into being, although he now knew every wrinkle in the gray cheek and around her mouth by heart, and often caressed her velvet nose and slipped her long ears between his fingers. But he still could not get her out in the morning without a prolonged struggle. Was it sheer cussedness on her part?

No, Andy became convinced that she was trying to tell him something, and he observed her closely, feeling his way through a dark tunnel of non-communication to what she meant. He noticed that whenever she came out of her stall into the barn proper, she sniffed around greedily for any bits of straw or hay she could find. What was she after? The Crockers had said clearly "a few handfuls of oats at night and morning and a pail of water." Had they forgotten something? Or was this balkiness to do, somehow, only with her sore ankles?

Lacking understanding, unable to speak her language, it was time, Andy thought, to call for medical advice. He had dreams of a happy donkey, kicking up her heels and racing down the field, of a donkey whose ears pricked forward and who trotted out each morning eagerly, of a donkey who no longer wheezed and uttered muffled oaths but who would give out with loud, joyful brays. The very idea of such a donkey made him smile ironically as he rubbed Whiffenpoof down with fly ointment for the nth time and she stood there, head bent, ears drooping, her lower lip thrust out with a look of disgust, then moved off before he had finished the job.

"Well, at least she knows her own mind," Andy thought. "At least she is independent."

He called the local vet, Dr. Bard. The voice was reassuring. Just the idea of an expert on the way to advise him made Andy feel more hopeful. But what he could not measure was how much, already, of the deadly inertia and introversion of depression had been lifted, even by the presence of a despondent and arthritic animal with whom he, so far, had failed to commune. A magic animal indeed!

That morning Andy played around with a humorous poem about a balky poet and the anger that held him back from the rich green meadows outside. It got going so well that by the end of the morning he was pacing up and down, unlit pipe in his pocket, reciting it, a long litany of complaints and curses, a nonsense poem which he found, at least for the moment, hilarious. He read it to Pussel, nothing daunted by the fact that, of course, only he laughed. Pussel narrowed her golden eyes and listened like a critic.

At this point Andy came back to practical reality, remembering Whiffenpoof's carrot and her lump of sugar. For once she greeted him with pricked ears and a rather noisier gasping whiffle than usual. She even nipped his sleeve in a playful way. Altogether it was a cheerful morning.

Early in the afternoon Dr. Bard drove up in a pale-green Cadillac, a stocky man with a lionesque head and a beaming smile, exuding confidence. He hardly waited to hear

Andy's explanations, but moved right out into the field with Whiffenpoof, patted her flank, and then quite casually picked up that dangerous back leg and felt along the shinbone and ankle.

"Yes, she's arthritic all right. See that swelling? It's common, you know, when these animals stand in the damp all winter."

He set the leg down, and gave Andy a piercing look as if to measure his understanding of the total situation.

"The Crockers take good care of their animals, but they're not rich. We could try cortisone while she's with you. It won't cure her—nothing will—but she'll feel less pain, and so will put more weight on her feet and enjoy life a little more."

"I'm willing," Andy said. "Of course I'm not exactly rich, but—well, I'd like to see her run!"

Dr. Bard looked at him quizzically.

"Tell you what—try half instead of a whole package of the powders I am going to leave with you, mixed with her oats once a day. I think it will do the trick."

Andy's purse was twenty dollars lighter when the Cadillac drove off but he couldn't count the cost *now*. It was too late for that. And his relief and gratitude were very great because Dr. Bard had listened with real attention about the balking and had suggested an explanation.

"Try some hay in the stall. She's used to that and she may miss it, in spite of all this lovely stuff here."

So that was it! Of course that must be the answer! And Andy dashed off in the Chevy before the dust from the Cadillac had settled. He must find someone who would deliver bales of hay. Why hadn't the Crockers told him? Maybe they had thought it was too much to ask, or maybe it never occurred to them that he wouldn't have provided it as a matter of course. In some ways the Crockers were as shy as wild animals; also they were proud people. They did not like to ask for anything.

That night Whiffenpoof was no longer deprived. She stood munching happily before a pile of sweet-smelling hay full of clover, and she stood on sawdust, for the man at the Farmer's Exchange had suggested that Andy invest in a bale or two of that. "It's cheap, and a real help in keeping the stall clean."

Well, it had taken more than a week for Andy to learn Whiffenpoof's basic needs, and she had, he thought, on the whole shown exemplary patience. She had never kicked or bitten him as he himself might have done to someone who deprived him of pipe tobacco for days and days. He stroked her nose tenderly when he left her in her bower of hay, and went peacefully to bed, just barely aware, as the night flowed past, of an occasional wheeze or stamping of hoofs out there in the barn.

"Dear thing," he murmured then, grateful to whatever powers had stayed his hand when, so often, he had wanted to beat her when she balked; when, instead, he had subdued the rage and had stood patiently at her side. In that visionary state between dream and waking he gave a long sigh. How often, in human affairs, just such a simple misunderstanding of motive or need causes all the pain and anger! Because we have words we think we can explain ourselves to each other, but how often words fail—the

elusive fish of personal truth slipping through them un-
seen and unheard. But, Andy thought, in a relation with
an animal we are back in the good wordless world which
tests our naked sensitivity. Intuition, sensing, is everything.
And as he slipped back into sleep, he promised Whiffenpoof to try to be more aware from now on, to learn her
language as best he could.

Whiffenpoof Has Some Fun

CHAPTER 8

One of the things Andy learned, as he became more expert in the language of donkey, was that Whiffenpoof was not an early riser. She wanted to be left in peace for an hour or two to enjoy her oats and some slow munching of fresh hay before she went out to the meadow. So, instead of trying to get her in motion by eight, Andy fed her and cleaned up the stall, and gave her a brush-off to get sawdust and hay out of her thick hair, then went in and had his breakfast, and took her out to the meadow only after he had done an hour's work at his desk. She is a sensible animal, he realized, far more sensible than I am for by ten of course the dew had dried and those sensitive ankles avoided getting wet.

These days she only pretended to balk, as a form of

flirtation or because she saw some succulent piece of clover en route that she simply could not do without. On the whole she followed Andy, docile though never slavish, in past the gate and stood there with a rather queenly air as he rubbed her down.

"There now," he said, giving her thigh a gentle slap. "O.K.?"

She turned her huge shaggy head and gave him a slow dark look, and as he walked toward the house, she went to the fence, ears forward, to watch him to the door, sometimes blowing a rather tender whiffle his way.

They had reached a kind of understanding at last, firm rather than passionate. Whiffenpoof reserved passionate interest for other animals and for children. When a family of summer neighbors moved back in July for weekends, she spent the whole morning standing in the corner of the field closest to their house and made loud wheezes, whiffles, and strangled brays, meant no doubt to be enticing. Judy and Jack were entranced, and ran over after breakfast with half a blueberry muffin or a piece of toast with marmalade on it, which Whiffenpoof accepted with careful soft lips. Their old spaniel, Molly, much too fat, was in a state of emotional confusion compounded of jealousy, curiosity, and playfulness before the new playmate. She rushed at the fence with muffled growls, but at the other end her tail was wagging furiously. If Whiffenpoof moved a muscle, she fled, howling, tail between her legs. All these attentions were accepted by the large gray animal with grave pleasure. But she was only really excited, Andy observed, when the Crockers went by, especially when they brought the team down. Then, moments before they were in sight, Whiffenpoof was pacing about close to the fence, lifting her head, nostrils wide open, ears forward, uttering loud brays of affection and recognition.

She must be feeling better, Andy decided, because she was now, at last, able to utter honest-to-goodness brays, and since she obviously enjoyed the sound of her own voice, she brayed a good deal, especially when she thought it was time for elevenses.

One morning Andy was in a hurry and forgot to rub her down. When he went out at eleven, the ineffable animal was standing at the gate, holding the bright-blue plastic pail in her mouth by its handle, her tail swinging furiously, with a rather smug expression on her face. Andy was so delighted that he ran to hug her head, pail and all.

"What a clever girl!" he said, as he went swiftly to work to make more of the mixture, and then to rub Whiffenpoof down. He could see horrible black flies clinging in the thick hair under her belly.

"Awful, aren't they?" he said, stopping to brush one off his own forehead, "but we'll be out of the woods in another week or so, old thing."

But just then—a fly must have got through to a tender place—she suddenly wheeled, kicked up her heels, and raced down the field. Well!—Andy was astonished—so she could do *that* now! The cortisone was indeed "doing the trick." Andy felt deep-down satisfaction. He felt comforted. But this comfort had cost a lot of hard work, many interruptions to his writing, and the rather scary ebbing of his bank account. Whiffenpoof was proving a distraction all right—a charming distraction—but she consumed a hell of a lot of time. Andy thought, with wry amusement, that it was she who was leading the life of a poet and he, the life of a donkey, fetching, carrying, cleaning up, brushing, rubbing down, forking hay, while she mused in her pasture without a care in the world!

"Something to take care of" was only a partial answer to filling the hole left by Miss Hornbeam's disregard. After all, he had had no wish to "take care of" the Muse. Her function was to inspire. In this respect, so far, Whiffenpoof was rather a failure. Somewhere inside him there was still an empty space which nothing, not even the dear gray face and the marvelous long ears, inhabited.

Yet there were intimations—moments when something stirred Andy's heart—when, for instance, he went into the barn occasionally after dark to have a last little chat. Then sometimes he could not feel a soft nose waiting to be caressed in the window of the stall, but if he looked in he could just distinguish Whiffenpoof lying down, head bent. The dear creature, asleep there, so vulnerable and alone, spoke to Andy of patience and tenderness and long-suffering, and he felt strangely moved, and close to poetry. But by morning the moment of feeling had vanished. There was no sustained hum of music in his head.

Of course it was a time when much outdoor work needed to be done. He was preoccupied with that. The rainy June had made the garden flourish in a jungly way, including massive numbers of healthy weeds. The vegetable patch was in need of hoeing. Whenever Andy sat down to work, he began to remember chores he might well be at, and this was a sure sign that he was not on the beam as far as his work at the desk went. Whenever a shadowy Hornbeam floated into his mind, he banged down his fist and said "Whiffenpoof" aloud, but it did not always work, for Miss Hornbeam still exerted a powerful spell. Something is missing, he thought, and it is surely joy. What joy meant for Andy was being related to something, to someone, a being who could call out the poet and make him dance again. Whiffenpoof had not, after all, given him back the sense of himself that he had lost, the boy on a tightrope who was hidden somewhere deep in the old man. Perhaps we are too much alike, Andy thought. These days he often felt like a donkey himself.

He was in a pretty disconsolate mood when he went out that afternoon to take Whiffenpoof in for her oats and water. She was, as always these days, waiting eagerly at the gate, bumping her head against it and expressing quite clearly that it was time her master—or her servant—paid a little attention to her needs. Quite mechanically, in a routine gesture, Andy lifted the hook and flung the gate wide. Then it happened—before he could get a hold on the halter, Whiffenpoof veered, made a nimble caper, back legs flung out, and streaked off straight for the garden.

"No . . . no!" Andy called, "not that way, girl! Not the lettuces . . ." and by quick moving he managed to turn her off. She gave him a wary glance, then nonchalantly trotted off past the house and onto the road. There she slowed down, hesitated, and only when she was sure he would follow, made another erratic run—a highland fling, Andy thought, chuckling. Then, when she felt at a safe distance, she stopped to nibble at the tender green leaves of a bush. By now, of course, Andy had caught onto the game, that it was indeed a game, and he played it happily, laughing so much he was quite out of breath.

At this point Tom drove past in his pick-up, took in the hilarous scene, and slowed down.

"Want some help?"

"Oh no," Andy called. "Let her run! It's good for her. I'll catch her sooner or later."

Meanwhile, intoxicated by her new freedom, Whiffen-poof went tearing up the hill toward the cemetery.

"I'm not going to run up that hill, my girl," Andy panted.

After all, why not let her have her highland fling? She *meant* to be followed—that was clear in the way she waited for him fifty yards or so ahead. And what a heavenly sight it was, the twinkle of her slender legs, the sudden gambols and capers of the enclosed and imprisoned at last free from pain, free from walls, free! She seemed to be led by her own ears, held far forward, ready for adventure, and just now they led her to turn in at the driveway of a very well-kept, prim summer place. Good heavens, what if she started to eat one of the Hamptons' rare bushes? Or kicked a hole in the immaculate, freshly raked driveway?

Andy did run then, but strategy was in order, and he had the wit not to try a direct approach but swung around the house to trap her if possible where she stood in front of the garages. Andy was coming in from behind her, slowly now, trying to make no sound, but just as he got within reach of her tail, one ear flew back and off she ran, kicking up her heels. Then, quite suddenly, she stopped, eyeing Andy with a calm eye, demure as a demoiselle. This time, for reasons known only to herself, she let Andy come right up and take the halter, nuzzled at his sleeve, and let him stroke her head between the ears.

"Well, we've had quite a caper. But now, my friend, you are coming home to your oats, willy-nilly," said Andy firmly.

He couldn't keep the smile off his face as they walked down the hill, Andy in the lead, Whiffenpoof, sedate and willing, at his heels. For the dream was really coming true, the dream of Andy and a donkey taking a peaceful walk together on a fine summer day.

When Whiffenpoof was firmly tied up in her stall, and before he got out the oats, Andy stood there beside her and put one arm around her, so the gray head leaned against his shoulder for a second. He felt extremely happy —for what he had foreseen rather grimly only a few hours ago as a long summer of chores, a melancholy andante of a lame donkey and a deluded old man, had turned suddenly into a scherzo, a summer of escapades and adventures, a summer of the running away of Whiffenpoof in the afternoon. This was more like it!

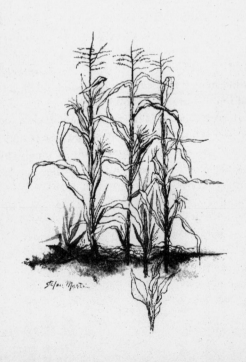

Afternoons of a Donkey

CHAPTER 9

There is something faintly ridiculous, no doubt, about an elderly gentleman chasing a donkey up hill and down dale, a donkey who is a born tease and who knows that her pursuer can't win. But Andy did not mind being ridiculous because he was enjoying himself so much. After all, this was his dream come true of a loving, carefree, and well donkey, an ornery, delightful companion full of whim and fancy.

In the afternoon of Whiffenpoof's first escape, it happened by chance that Judy and Jack had gone for a swim; old Mr. Purl was indoors; and Mrs. Dear's little granddaughter, Tabitha, was off somewhere on her bicycle; so Andy had had the village to himself, unobserved. But, as the days followed each other in the mood of the scherzo, four o'clock in the afternoon became donkey-tag time, and soon numbers of children and people of all ages gathered in the chase, and Andy could look on himself as a beneficent magician who, every day, opened the gate into joy.

Whiffenpoof, meanwhile, was becoming more daring in her discovery of avenues of escape. One of the best was around the schoolhouse and up the steep hill to old Mr. Purl's; he had stopped her in front of his door the first time she tried it, with his arms flung wide like some Old Man of the Mountain, and Whiffenpoof chose to challenge him again on later outings. Andy's only fear was that she would take the winding downhill road to the next village, for he did not enjoy the idea of hauling her all that way back uphill, when and if she was caught. So he posted the children here and there at strategic spots to head her in the right direction.

Of course some people did not have a clue as to what this was all about.

"If you held the halter firmly when you opened the gate, she wouldn't run away," the kindly mailman suggested, as one might try to protect a gentle lunatic.

"Oh, but I want her to run away," Andy answered without showing a flicker of amusement. "That's the whole point."

"I see," said Mr. Meacham, thoroughly mystified. "She's supposed to do it, is she?" And he took off his cap to scratch his head.

"Well, she has arthritis, you know, and running is good for her ankles." It was crystal clear to Andy.

When Mrs. Packer, just back for the summer, asked him to tea he had to refuse of course. "Sorry, but at four the donkey runs away and I have to be at home to catch her."

"That man is pulling my leg," Mrs. Packer said to her husband. "I have three copies of his new book for him to sign, too. He just won't come—looks down on us, I suppose," for Mr. Packer had made his fortune in soap and Mrs. Packer was always on the lookout for a snub.

"Nothing to stop your taking the books down there at four, is there?" Mr. Packer was practicing putting on the vast living-room carpet. "Then you can see whether he is pulling your leg or not."

So the chauffeur and the Lincoln Continental were at the door at four the next afternoon, and off they went down to the village to see what was what.

"Soames, I want you to park on the green and stay there. I understand there may be a happening."

The green had lately been enclosed in a low white fence and looked a little like a paddock, and there Soames glided the big car to a halt, with Mrs. Packer inside keeping an eye on Andy's meadow. There indeed was a donkey, butting her head against the gate, then backing off to look longingly toward the house, her ears pricked. When Andy himself came out in a bright red shirt, the donkey gave a loud bray. Judy and Jack appeared at their door as if at a signal, while Mr. Purl just happened to be standing in front of his house trimming a vine. It was a moment of considerable suspense as Andy, unhurried, smiling his secret smile, walked up to the gate and unfastened it.

At once Whiffenpoof bolted, kicked up her heels two

or three times in a saucy way, veered toward the garden and was out of Mrs. Packer's sight for a moment (although she could hear Andy shouting), and then reappeared, coming out lickety-split toward the green.

"Good heavens, that donkey is running away, sure enough!" Mrs. Packer said to Soames. "Whatever has that man thought up now?"

Andy had long ago given up running, it just got him out of breath.

"Let her go!" he called out to the children who had scampered after her shouting, "Stop Whiffenpoof!"

And then he noticed the Lincoln Continental poised there like a shining dark-green insect, and sauntered casually over. Whiffenpoof meanwhile had given the car a rather wild look, had sprung over the fence, and was absorbed in devouring the luscious thick grass inside.

"Good afternoon, Mrs. Packer," Andy said as she rolled down her window by pushing a button. "You have come for the games, I see. We have them every afternoon now —livens things up, wouldn't you say?"

"Well, I never!"

Just at that instant, Whiffenpoof, who had not lifted her head but whose ears told her that Andy was getting rather too close, danced off again, over the fence and up the hill, pausing once to be sure she was being followed.

"It's a chase," Andy explained. "I have to go—sorry!" And off he went at a gentle jog, calling back, "Head her off, kids, if you can"—a thing they were only too eager to do.

It was a wild scramble up the hill back of the little library, but head her off they did, and she came careening down again and out onto the main road. This was a dangerous ploy because of possible through traffic, and Andy had to run now, after all. He reached the middle of the road just as a huge van came charging into the village and ground to a halt before the innocent and wily Whiffenpoof, who had decided to make a stand there.

Andy was so out of breath between laughing and running that he could not speak.

"Hey, what is this, a circus?" the driver shouted, furious at this crazy impediment to traffic. "Get that animal out of my way!"

But nothing could be happier, as far as Andy was concerned, than forcing a lumbering, noisy giant of a truck to halt in its tracks like a baffled dragon, and he was not going to hurry. When he had caught his breath he said serenely, "She'll move when she has a mind to."

The driver bore down heavily on his horn, apparently speechless with rage, and Whiffenpoof, startled by this unlikely sound, lifted her head and brayed as loudly as she could. The furious driver blew his horn again, and so the dialogue continued for some moments. Whiffenpoof was obviously delighted by this chance to insult a truck, and she had the last word. Then, for no reason at all, she sauntered slowly off to the side of the road, paying not the slightest heed to the screechings and groanings of the monster as it got up speed again and disappeared in a cloud of dust and black fumes.

"Soames, get out and catch that donkey before it gets killed," Mrs. Packer commanded, and the obedient Soames joined the chase. Whiffenpoof, inspired by all this attention, had now taken a new tack, and was disappearing behind old Mrs. Prin's barn. Mrs. Packer could no longer see what was happening. She heard a muffled oath from Soames, as, no doubt, the beast eluded his grasp. Andy and the children too had disappeared behind the barn. Curiosity got the better of her, and she emerged, advancing with all deliberate speed just as Whiffenpoof, trumphant, ran out again. Taken aback by this new and formidable player on her stage, the donkey came to a halt, nostrils flaring and breathing hard, just a foot from Mrs. Packer.

"I've got her!" she cried, taking a firm hold on the halter.

She stood there in a whirl of children, Andy, Soames, and even old Mrs. Prin, who all came to congratulate Whiffenpoof as if she were an Olympic athlete who had just broken her own record, and, rather as an afterthought, congratulated Mrs. Packer for her clever catch.

Then they all tagged along after Andy as he led the now tranquil and biddable creature home and into the barn, Mrs. Packer far in the rear but determined to see this event to its conclusion.

"Soames," she called, "get the books out of the car!"

"You must admit it's fun," Andy said, shining with the good cheer of it all, for who could have imagined that the formidable Mrs. Packer, of all people, would not only catch Whiffenpoof but come right into the barn and show such an interest in all his arrangements?

"What made you do it—borrow a donkey?" she asked when Whiffenpoof had been fed and watered, the children dispersed, and they were in Andy's house so that he could sign the books.

"I don't know," Andy said as he searched for a pen, "quiet desperation, I guess."

On any other occasion he would never have said anything as self-revealing to Mrs. Packer, but then he had never liked her before. In the presence of Whiffenpoof, everyone became more human, and that was one of her charms, so even Mrs. Packer (of all people!) had come under the good spell, he thought, and was almost likable.

She, meanwhile, was looking around this solitary man's lair in much the way she had looked around the barn, with hungry curiosity.

"You keep everything awfully neat, Mr. Lightfoot."

"I can't work in a muddle." Andy signed his name and the date with a flourish and handed the books over. "Kind of you to buy these. Did you like the poems?"

He could not imagine that she had even glanced at them, for it was an axiom that people in Lincoln Continentals do not read poetry. He was being polite.

"These are Christmas presents," she said.

"Yes, well," Andy said with a twinkle, "Christmas is a long way off. You might just steal a read between now and then."

"Poetry scares me," Mrs. Packer confessed with unexpected candor.

"Why does it scare you?" Andy was truly interested in this large, frightened, self-conscious creature before him. "Oh, do sit down! Let me make you a cup of tea . . ."

"Just for a minute, but no tea, thank you," and she sank

into the big armchair, rather tense still, he felt.

"A glass of sherry? A small Scotch and soda?"

It was a perilous moment, Andy thought as he came round from behind his desk, the moment of contact, the moment when a door opens between two people who have been acquaintances for years but never managed or cared to open the door. The fact is, Andy had not wanted to. He had pigeonholed Mrs. Packer among the very rich, whom he regarded, like administrators, as people who could not afford to be quite human. Now he persuaded her gently to have a "small Scotch." He set a match to the fire and there they were, sitting opposite each other, almost like old friends. He sensed that behind the matronly figure, the heavy jowls and the tight little mouth, she was full of tremors, a very delicate and sensitive machine, afraid of its own power to register distant earthquakes.

"Why does poetry scare you? Do tell me," he begged. "It might help."

"I don't know how it could help you," and she laughed shyly. "I guess I'm afraid I won't understand it." She caught Andy's penetrating look. "Or if I did, it might hurt. I try to keep away from things that upset me."

"But how can you? Life is upsetting, isn't it?"

"Oh yes, I suppose so."

Mrs. Packer looked quite distraught and took a sip of her drink, then quite a gulp, as she gazed into the fire.

"Sometimes a poem can make the unbearable bearable . . . or so I have found."

"But you must get lonely sometimes. It can't be easy."

"Loneliness isn't the problem," Andy adventured. "It is

that sometimes I can't light the fire—I can't write poems."

"Then what do you do?"

"This time I borrowed a donkey!"

"Has it worked?"

"Has it? I wonder . . ." Andy mused. "I've had a lot of fun anyway."

They were listening to each other through the words, Andy thought, so he was not surprised when Mrs. Packer appeared to change the subject, still looking into the fire and only now and then directly at him.

"It's not easy for anyone, getting older," she said. "I used to play tennis rather well . . . you wouldn't believe it, would you?" and it was indeed hard to imagine this huge heaviness running lightly about a tennis court. But Andy waited for what she really wanted to say, and finally she murmured, "After our son was killed in that crazy automobile accident, I got fat. Something died in me."

They looked into the fire together. Andy had been listening so hard that he forgot to say anything, but she did not appear to mind. Nor did he feel compelled. Understanding flowed between them.

"It *is* harder getting older," he said then out of what he had been thinking. "More seems to be asked and we have less to give. We know too much in one way—there are fewer saving graces." Then he chuckled. "I'm heavy, too, and it slows me down, but you know what? I like to think that it makes me look solid, someone to lean on . . . who wants to be fashionable? There's something to be said for an old mountain, but very little to be said for an old clotheshorse, don't you agree?"

Mrs. Packer laughed, and Andy realized that when she laughed she looked suddenly very endearing and that laughter was her way of giving herself away.

"I *am* a solitary," he went on, "but the poetry comes from somewhere, has to be attached to something. Whiffenpoof has been a kind of attachment, I suppose."

He shot Mrs. Packer a quick glance, but she was not laughing at him so he went on.

"Absurd, of course. But, you see, I had waited so very long—three years—for a word from a human attachment. I had to invent something, foolish man that I am."

He got up and walked up and down.

"Will you read the poems? Please do."

"I guess I'll have to." She uttered one of her sudden inappropriate laughs.

One reason that Andy led a solitary life, he considered, was that as soon as he met another human being for even a brief moment, he gave himself away. It was a congenital hazard of being a poet, maybe, since poetry demands that one keep oneself absolutely transparent into old age, and, so, vulnerable beyond what is considered grown-up. But he could not afford to do this too much or too often. As it was, he felt increasingly tied down by a huge web of all the people who thought of him as an intimate friend because they had once had a cup of coffee together at a bus station in Kalamazoo.

Mrs. Packer watched him pacing up and down and imagined that he was wrapped in some deep thought which had no possible connection with her presence there.

She got up.

"I must be going. Thank you so much for signing the

books."

Andy stopped short, bewildered.

"Sorry," he said, coming to. "It's nice to be friends after all these years."

"Yes," she said, taking his offered hand and shaking it with surprising warmth. "It's nice."

Andy watched her walk slowly out to the car and drive off, and he was smiling because it had never occurred to him that a wild creature could inhabit a Lincoln Continental and be driven home by a chauffeur. What would she make of the poems? He opened one of his books at random and read two or three through her eyes, seeing them freshly, and as usual when this happened, was thoroughly dissatisfied. He really must write a poem for this touching old creature, for her alone.

Mrs. Packer's visit, opening up so much so unexpectedly, had excited him. After she had gone, he felt restless and went out to the barn, as he often did these days, for a quiet conversation with Whiffenpoof. She was munching hay and gave him a rather cynical look, or so he imagined. He read so much into her—sometimes he wondered if she read anything into him.

"I've grown accustomed to your face," he sang, stroking her nose, and he noticed that she had a sparse beard under that stubborn lower lip so much like his own.

It was wonderfully quieting here in the barn. Andy stood for some minutes in the door, looking out into the green light of evening—the leaves had lost their transparency and had become opaque screens, never entirely still. But it was a fresh, alive world just the same, full of promise. He counted five different bird songs while he stood there, two of which he did not recognize. The swallows zigzagged in and out over his head, twittering at this unaccustomed presence in their regular flight pattern. Then a pair of bluebirds flew down and began to pick at the gravel, the first he had seen this year. That startling blue, as unreal as the wings of an angel, always made him catch his breath. It felt like a good augury.

For all this dawdling about and Whiffenpoof-talk was only because a poem was rising . . . he could feel it, a restless stir inside him which had no definition yet, and no words attached to it. He was not starting from words now, but from somewhere below the level of consciousness. He must have stood a half hour there in the barn doorway, and when he went indoors it was twilight and he sat at his desk in a state of luminosity—like the fireflies, he thought, who had begun to pulse their signals in the grass as he walked across the garden to come in.

In this state, he came to understand that what had touched him about Mrs. Packer was that she had invented no role in life for herself. She was absolutely vulnerable. So they had recognized each other. Having no role, no image of herself to live by, she was miserable of course. She was like a snail with no shell.

Just as I have been lately, Andy realized. He realized, too, in this hour of exceptional aliveness, that it was a long while since he had felt the demon of rage trying to take him over. Anger was withering away inside him. But he could not have said why this was, or what had really been happening since Whiffenpoof started running away.

A Thunderstorm

CHAPTER 10

They had, lately, had a respite from the rain, and the air had been luminous indeed, washed clean, all the various greens bursting clear in a stained-glass radiance. But the next day Andy woke to purple and black clouds pouring down from the northwest, and he hesitated—should he keep Whiffenpoof in her stall? Well, after all, he could run back with her if the storm broke, so he decided finally to take her out. The clouds might be only wind clouds, after all.

He was longing to get to work, to make a start at that new poem, a shadowy presence still, but he decided to hold out against its stirrings, not try to capture anything so elusive, but allow it to seize him when it was ready. Instead he pulled out the rough drafts of a translation of

Odilon-Jean Périer's poem "La Route," feeling a new impetus, almost an obligation to bring this poem out into English, whole. He had been working at it, off and on, for months. It presented great difficulties. Yet it had continued to haunt. The Belgian poet had died young, had known, possibly, that he was dying when he had composed it. Andy Lightfoot was close to old age and perfectly well, yet the poem spoke to him intimately. He wished he had written it himself. This morning he sat down to give it one more try, with his attention honed to a sharp, bright edge.

This peace, this marvelous star, poignant and bright,
The ship, all sails unfurled, of every night,
        Song's hidden beat—
Like a man wandering his own house, his tower,
I step through all the secrets of this hour
        On desperate feet.

I yield up all the tenderest images,
Change paths, change countries, even languages,
        Only to find what has been always here—
A street where sky lets down its gentle lees,
        Old airs and poetries,
My love's hands and the changing atmosphere.

Always the same man, the same mystery,
Those shining bursts of joy or sudden fury,
        Plans, recollection—
When, strong enough for silence, shall I live,—not ask
        For book or mask—
Landscape or mirror, true to your reflection?

When he had torn up and re-begun the first three stanzas innumerable times, Andy remembered Whiffenpoof, and at noon went out with a carrot for her. Today, after all, not she but poetry had made the world stand still—three hours had passed in what seemed a few minutes. Luckily the magic animal did not seem to have noticed that he was late. She had taken up her vigil at the corner and was absorbed in watching a game of touch football across the road. Andy, coming into the light from hours of concentration, felt quite dazzled. A sunbeam touched an Indian paintbrush and made it glow like fire. The clouds had not blown over. The sky was a troubled, towering mass of dark and light, a drama in itself, and he stood for some moments looking at it. Then he went for a little walk around the garden and came back bearing a huge pink Papaver poppy like a trophy in his hand. How admirable, he thought, was its sturdy, hairy stem, and the brittle cup of the bud which those diaphanous pleated petals had forced back, as they opened wide to show the strength and richness of the crown of purple stamens at their center. Andy did not often pick flowers. He was not an expert arranger, and then often forgot to change the water. Besides he liked to see them in their natural habitat. But today, as he had known from the beginning, was to be momentous. He set the poppy alone in a tall glass on his desk like some magic presence. You are there, he thought, and I am here, and we are both absorbed in the work of creation. In a day or so one of those great butterfly wings would drop off, and then another, until the hieratic seed pod stood alone, as sturdy and apparently impregnable as the petals had been fragile and given to change. So the flower was not as still as it looked, and might be thought of as performing an infinitely slow dance toward fruition, just as he, Andy, sat absolutely still for hours, holding the motion of a poem in his hands, filled with the joy of the struggle.

It occurred to him, when he took time out for a pipe and had swallowed down a glass of milk, that the young man who had written this poem, so filled with the urgency of living against despair, must also have felt joy as he wrote, for creation is joy even when it deals with excruciating truth.

> *But we must finish building in the gloom,*
> *Harvest some treasure from the shadowy room,*
> > *Or, lost there, kneel.*
> *I have not lived, my work is full of death!*
> *I hold your wrists, I listen to your breath.*
> *Love, passing love, what can you do to heal?*
>
> *Each day becomes more moving, fresh, and new—*
> *But why pick roses, they are mortal too?*
> *What can you leave less fleeting than the snow?*
> *Keep us from spoiling the divine Countenance!*
> *Let everything stay pure as it was once,*
> *As beautiful and sad as it is now.*
>
> *Let me return to your wise hands at last*
> *A seamless self in your own image cast,*
> *That your creation, God, not have to bear*
> *The ardor of this flesh, its fragile mark,*

Lost footsteps on the sand and through the dark,
This fall, these steps ... the footsteps of despair ...

It was past four when Andy had made the last correction and run a final draft through the typewriter of those difficult last stanzas. He had not lifted his head for an hour, so he was startled, when he did, to see that the world outside had turned ominously dark. Good heavens, the storm had really built up and was about to burst overhead. He had better hurry to get Whiffenpoof in before the downpour.

He ran out to the field without waiting to put on a jacket, and saw Whiffenpoof at the gate, weaving her head back and forth. She stopped as the door banged behind him and gave a strangled bray as he approached.

"Well, well," Andy laughed, "can't you do better than that, Whiffenpoof? You sound as if you had laryngitis."

He swung the gate back with every intention this time of holding onto her—it was no moment for a chase, God knows.

This was not Whiffenpoof's wish. And Whiffenpoof had become a very strong beast. She paid no attention at all to Andy's hand on the halter, just brushed him aside, shook her head, wheeled in a bold half circle away from him, and was off down the driveway before he recovered his balance, and just as a distant clap of thunder came rolling over the hills. Worse, she turned *down* the road this time, a thing he and the children had always managed to prevent on every other afternoon.

Where were they all? For once there wasn't a child in

sight. Here Andy made the fatal mistake of running. Whiffenpoof had been ambling slowly along, her ears forward, but as soon as she heard his footsteps coming up fast, she broke into a trot, and disappeared round a bend as the first heavy drops of rain began to fall. A loud clap of thunder was followed by a streak of lightning over the barn.

"Oh hell," Andy murmured, laughing half-heartedly at his plight, "she would do this in a storm!"

There was obviously no point in running. He would just have to call on his new-found patience and approach her quietly. After all, she might decide to come home when torrents of rain fell on her gray head and ears.

So Andy walked—down the hill, around bend after bend—and each time he came anywhere near, Whiffenpoof trotted off again. They had traveled a good mile down the winding road when the world grew so dark it felt like the middle of the night. Thunder sounded like cannon a few yards away. Now it was a downpour. Andy could hardly see. Now he was *not* laughing—he was wet and anxious.

Just as he had again lost sight of Whiffenpoof, a car stopped and a stranger leaned out to offer him a lift.

"Oh, thanks." Andy wiped the rain out of his eyes. "I'm after a donkey. She's round the next bend, I think."

"A donkey, eh?" The man looked amused. "Well, you're pretty wet. Maybe I could get past her and head her off. Want me to give it a try?"

"That would be very kind," Andy said with as much dignity as he could muster. He could feel water trickling down the legs of his jeans, down his neck and back, and

his sneakers plopped as he walked. But he was, he discovered, rather enjoying himself—even enjoying this ex-
hibition of extreme weather, for as they exchanged these
few words a shattering clap of thunder deafened them
both. The man gave a reassuring wave and eased off, while
Andy followed as fast as he could, a very wet jogger on
an involuntary outing.

Sure enough, round the next bend he saw the car set
crosswise and Whiffenpoof approaching it warily. The
man jumped out, and by the time Andy came up, soaking,
breathless, he was holding the halter.

"Well," Andy said, puffing, "you're a genius. Thank you!
Now I can lead her home."

"Good luck!" the man called as he backed the car swiftly
around and tore off.

Andy and Whiffenpoof now walked sedately back up
the hill in a companionable silence, Andy at first holding
onto the halter itself, but then, as Whiffenpoof had become
quite docile, taking the lead and pulling her along by the
rope. Whiffenpoof had turned dark gray in the wet. Water
trickled down her cheeks. Andy's shirt clung to his bones
like a wet bathing suit, as did his jeans, and he might as
well have been naked. He was chuckling again, amused
by this image of himself, looking like an old gypsy as he
dragged the long-eared beast behind him up the hill. And
it did seem a very long hill indeed. They moved through
curtains of heavy rain. The road itself was now a shallow
river, and they were going against the current. It was still
thundering and lightning, loud sinister cracks and blind-
ing flashes that made Andy jump and Whiffenpoof lay

back her ears.

He felt nervous, but elated, and very much alive. It had been a particularly splendid day from the start, he was thinking, as the patient bowed head nodded behind him, so this grand finale seemed entirely appropriate. More— he now had the feeling, for some reason, of having become entirely himself for the first time since the fatal meeting with Miss Hornbeam more than three years before. This absurd walk through a downpour, leading a donkey home, was exactly what he meant about his life. This, in some mysterious way, was *it*. If we have selves, he thought—and many people do not seem to—it is because each of us carries a secret image, a kind of mythical being buried somewhere under his ordinary appearance, a hero, per- haps, or a saint, or something quite different. It had been Miss Hornbeam's gift to him that for a time she had made it possible for this mythical being to emerge, the poet in all his naked and childlike innocence, and to function as a poet. She had brought a young boy back through all the years, to hope, to create, and, for good reason, to think well of himself. And the horror of her long silence had been that he had had to bear the slow fading away of the mythical being—the boy, the poet. So that, in that rainy June he had been left, he saw now, as bereft as Mrs. Packer after the death of her son, for surely her role had been maternal—and deprived of it she was nothing. Just as his role was to be a poet and deprived of it he became simply a crotchety, foolish old man. His innocence, his charity, had gone down the drain, and there was nothing to take their place.

But it was just his innocence and his charity that Whiffenpoof could use. He might have done something for Miss Hornbeam, perhaps, but like Mrs. Packer she was scared of poetry, so she could not accept the gift. It frightened her too much. What could she have done, Andy thought, wiping the rain off his eyelids for the hundredth time, with an old man's obsession? That, no doubt, was how she read it—for, after all, Miss Hornbeam belonged to the world. But Whiffenpoof was not mundane. "Are you, old thing?" he asked, leaning his wet cheek against her wet cheek as he paused an instant for breath.

They had at last reached the drive, and he turned in with relief for he had been a little anxious about Whiffenpoof's tender hoofs, so apt to pick up a pebble, so unused to hard macadam roads. Yes, he could do everything for this gentle, willful, dark-eyed piece of magic, he thought as he forked down a load of hay into her stall, wiped the rain off her eyelashes, and gave her a quick rubdown while she munched.

"You know, girl, I'm not so old as I once was!"

The boy, the gypsy, the poet had just had a splendid outing in Whiffenpoof's company. So he stroked her soft gray nose with particular tenderness when she pushed it through the window for that ritual caress.

The storm had clarified things. It had set everything back into proportion again for Andy, even to the insight that he did not have to keep Whiffenpoof forever. He could let her go when the summer was over. For he had done what he meant to do—made her well, able to run away and to have her joys, to be the complete, balky, whimsical animal she was meant to be. And she, meanwhile, had helped him recover his sense of himself: runner after the impossible on desperate—oh yes, sometimes desperate!—feet.

"Each day becomes more moving, fresh, and new"—and who wants to live outside pain, outside joy? Not Andy Lightfoot, the boy who borrowed a donkey for the summer, and the old man who had come to know why.